by

Beth Mitchell Stephenson

This is a work of fiction. All characters are fictional and any resemblance to persons living or dead is purely coincidental.

Cover art and design by Amie Jacobsen.

Library of Congress Catalog Card Number: 2002115151
Printed in the United States of America

First Edition: November 2002
Second Edition: November 2009

Dedicated to

Hal and Patricia Mitchell

Chapter 1

Starvation

Rocky lay still on the thin mattress, waiting to hear familiar voices so she could return to peaceful sleep.

"What is it?" The little girl heard Jamie's voice outside the window where she lay.

"It's Jack Daniels." The answering voice told her it was The Fat Man with the bald head and long beard. She expected it to be him from the roar of his motorcycle. The Fat Man had never come into the trailer, and her mother seemed to trust him. She listened to their murmured voices sometimes rising to laughter. The seven-year-old sat up and tried to straighten the scratchy blanket under her. It was too hot for a blanket in June, and, if Jamie came to bed before morning, she would lie on it the way it was. It would be too late to fix it.

The morning sun was already heating the tiny travel trailer when Rocky woke. Her mother was sprawled on the foot of the bed fully clothed, as the child expected. Her mouth was open, and the bare mattress was wet under her cheek. There were stains under her arms, and the mud crusted on the seat of Jamie's shorts didn't surprise her daughter. Flies on her face hardly rose as the little girl tried to shoo them away. It did not rouse Jamie. Rocky didn't want to wake her for she knew she would have a bad headache.

The waste tank was full in the tiny bathroom, and since the trailer was not hooked up to any sewer, there was nothing the child could do about it. She closed the lid on the toilet and slipped outside to relieve herself in the tall grass. Her mother had told her that the more she watered the grass the taller it would grow. The little room with walls of grass smelled much better than the trailer bathroom anyway. She checked herself for ticks, as Jamie had instructed, before reentering the trailer.

She rubbed her eyes, wondering why she had a headache when she hadn't tasted any of the bottles The Fat Man brought every night. Jamie had taken her to Sample Saturday at the grocery store the day before, but they hadn't bought anything. She thought she would feel better if she could find something to eat.

Rocky swung the door of the fridge open as far as she could without hitting her mother's feet. There was nothing but crumbs in the box of cornflakes, but after shaking the flies out of a dirty bowl, she dumped in the last of the cereal. The milk had tasted sour the day before, but she had saved just enough to moisten her cereal one more day. She wrinkled her nose as it came out in lumps and water. But her head pounded, and Jamie would tell her to eat something. She plugged her nose and swallowed a spoonful. Mom said that sour milk was just as good as sweet milk, but sour milk made your hair pretty. She tried a second bite but let go of her nose to shoo off a fly and was forced to spit it out. She had eaten the last soda cracker the day before, too, and she knew there were no more peanuts in her mother's purse.

The little girl slipped out of her summer nighty and pulled on her orange, knit shorts and the pink and orange-flowered shirt. She pirouetted in front of the narrow mirror. The shorts had been tight in May when they were new but now nearly slipped down over her bony hips. The front of the shirt and the seat of the shorts were gray from wear, but Rocky twisted as far as she could to see if the back was still pretty. She turned the shirt backward with the tag sticking up under her chin so the bright new-looking flowers were in front and decided it looked much better. She had three pairs of shorts and three shirts, all in the same condition. She had mended her rubber sandals with tape from her school kit, but the plastic flower wouldn't stay on anymore. When Grandma bought her summer clothes at the thrift store, she bought her new panties too and told her to put on a clean pair every day. But Grandma had not come over to see them for a long time, and no laundry had been done for several weeks. The little girl, willing to be good and do as she was told, switched her underwear every day anyway.

She brushed her pale hair out of her face, curling it a little with the brush. It was lighter in the summer, since she spent most of her time out of doors, and the part she could see in front did look pretty. Rocky had a gift for optimism, and she imagined it shimmering in golden curls down her back, the way it had when Grandma took her to get her picture taken at Christmas time. Her optimism spared her from suspecting that it was a mass of tangled fuzz on the back of her head.

The metal step was already hot when Rocky stepped outside. She skipped the second step so she wouldn't burn her feet. There was a shady place behind the trailer where she found the ground littered with the week's whiskey flasks. She gathered them up as usual, but when she tried to break them into the neighbor's trash can, she found her arms were heavy, and she had to try a second and third time before the first one would break. At last she gave up and dropped them in whole. Usually she enjoyed breaking the bottles, but the bright sun near the street made her eyes ache.

Suddenly, she squealed with pleasure as she noticed that a little nook made by the tree roots cradled a small bag of burnt peanut candy. She seized it, found it unopened and hugged the cellophane sack as though it was an over-flowing Easter basket. Somebody must have dropped it in the dark and couldn't find it between the roots. It did not occur to her that she often found little treats in the same place after The Fat Man visited.

She tucked the candy into the waistband of her shorts and scampered like a squirrel up a nearby tree. But when the empty bag fluttered to the ground a minute later, she leaned back with a soft groan. Her tummy hurt. It wasn't the usual gnawing emptiness, but a stabbing pain twisting her insides. The tree trunk felt solid and cool against her hot forehead, and she braced herself a little as her stomach tried to return the peanuts. She was too weak, even for that. If only she could sit down in the cool grocery store. She would ask for a sample of ice cream and lick it slowly. She tried to lie back but remembered that she was in the tree and shifted herself enough that she was wedged in the place where the tree divided. The bark chafed her back, but she told herself it was like a cradle. She drew up her knees and buried her head in her arms.

Rocky dozed feverishly until early afternoon when the pain in her belly overcame her weariness. Her mouth was dry, but her stomach was a hard knot. She didn't dare swallow anything, but at last her thirst drove her to try to get down from the tree.

The foot and handholds seemed further apart than she expected as she tried to climb down, and she couldn't see well. When she tried to focus her eyes, everything moved slowly to her left, like she was watching it pass from the window of a slow-moving car, and the light seemed to fade and return with the turning view. She tried to cling to the tree trunk as she descended, but she fell the last few feet. Her forearm hit a root, and pain flashed like fire. She raised her head. It seemed that her arm was crooked, but she didn't know what that meant. There was only pain and gathering darkness. She strained to find the trailer door, and when she did, she focused on it and pushed herself up with her uninjured arm. She tripped on the step and didn't bother to open her eyes as she crawled on one hand and her knees inside.

The little girl vaguely noticed the stifling heat indoors. Jamie slept sitting on the bed with her head and arms on the table. She must have gotten up and fallen asleep again. Rocky lay back on the head of the bed and whimpered,

"Mom, I'm sick."

There was a low groan. "What, baby?"

"I'm sick, and I hurt my arm."

"I know the feeling." She sat up and rubbed her own tangled hair, glancing outside to see the time of day. She stepped into the bathroom, plugging her nose. "It stinks so bad in here, I can taste it," she mumbled. She went outside, and when she returned to her seat on the bed, Rocky laid her right hand on her mother's thigh.

"Did Grandma come by?"

"No. I ate the candy and felt sick, and went to sleep in the tree. Then I hurt my arm." She lifted it with her other hand to show the purpling lump between her wrist and her elbow. "Do you think it's broken?" Her voice was so feeble that Jamie could barely understand her.

"Oh! Oh, no." She covered her mouth with her hand. "No, baby, it's just a bruise. I'm sorry you bruised your arm. I'll go get some food. Someone gave me some money yesterday, and I'll go get some Popsicles. Would that make you feel better?"

"I . . . I think I'm dying," She lay back on the twisted blanket, with her awareness gathering on pain and darkness. "I ate some candy."

"You shouldn't eat candy for breakfast."

"The milk was sour," she murmured.

"It will make your hair pretty."

She nodded slightly.

"That's my good baby." Jamie opened the cupboard. The cereal box was empty. The fridge was also empty. She saw the soggy cereal on the table and shooed the flies out of it. "I know it's nasty, but you better eat some more. There's nothing else."

"Sick."

Jamie pushed the spoon into her daughter's mouth. Rocky pushed it onto the mattress with her tongue, and shook her head faintly.

"It's better than nothing. Open up." Rocky had fallen into a vacant stupor. Jamie closed her eyes and rubbed her temples. Her headache raged, and she couldn't think. Rocky gagged, unknowing, and Jamie swept the burnt peanuts out of her daughter's mouth and wiped her fingers on the mattress.

Rocky stirred and opened her eyes. "Can I have some water?" Jamie read her lips more than she could hear what she said.

"Just a minute!" Her voice rose in pitch as she realized the water bottles were empty. Rocky usually filled them every morning, but they lay in the sink.

Rocky repeated, "Water,"

Jamie grabbed the bottles. "I'm going as fast as I can!" She turned on the outside spigot on the neighbor's trailer hookup and filled the water bottles. She jostled Rocky, holding out the bottle, but when Rocky didn't take it, she squirted it into her mouth. When the little girl licked her lips, she squirted a little more. "That's a good girl. You'll feel better when you have a drink." She tried not to look at the swelling, purplish lump on the arm that lay on the bare mattress.

Jamie sat with her head in her hands beside her daughter. "Grandma better get here soon."

Rocky moved her head up and down once. "Thank you, Mama," she murmured.

When Rocky woke, the trailer was dark. Her mind was clearer than it had been, and she noticed that the air was cooler and a breeze blew some of the oppressive odor out the open window. She called Jamie's name, knowing that if she didn't answer, she had gone to the store for some food. Nobody did answer. Rocky lifted the water bottle with her right hand, leaving her left arm resting. The pain in her arm was not as bad as before, but she didn't dare move it. *Or maybe Jamie went to get Grandma*, she thought.

As she became more alert, the pain in her stomach made her whimper. Her swollen arm throbbed. The breeze that had cooled her was too cold now, and she began to shiver. The blanket was twisted under her, but she knew she didn't have the strength to pull it over herself. The walls turned slowly around her like a playground merry-go-round grinding on its axis.

She dozed again, dreaming that the man who drove

the yellow car was cutting off her arm. She tried to wake, but the fog of delirium would not disperse. She saw the long, black hair of the man with the yellow car. He was sitting on her, and she could not breathe. Jamie's voice echoed as from a distant hallway and laughed or cried, but Rocky couldn't tell which. The man had a big knife and was going to stab her. The pain in her stomach was terrible.

Suddenly, the man disappeared, and her body relaxed. The pain in her arm vanished, and her stomach didn't hurt at all. She was light as a soap bubble and encircled by light. People who wore white clothes gathered around her, their faces and hair shining. They smiled and welcomed her as though they had been waiting for her to come. Though Rocky didn't recognize them, she wasn't afraid at all. Music, more beautiful than she had ever imagined, enveloped her, and filled her with perfect peace. Some of the people in white sang with the music, and it vibrated in her heart as though she was part of the instrument.

She wanted to cry, but she wasn't sad. She wanted to sing too, to be part of the great river of music, but the words were unfamiliar and hard to understand with her mind. Their song was love and longing, a joyful reaching with their voices. Rocky felt love too, and listened with her whole body so that she could understand and sing with them. She yearned to know the One they sang for.

But as she strained to comprehend, a woman knelt

down in front of her and took Rocky's face in her hands. She kissed her on both cheeks. "Not yet, sweetheart. It's not time for you to be here."

"No, please let me stay!" she begged. She felt the throbbing darkness behind her and strained harder to capture the song that caressed her. But the woman took her hand, patting it tenderly, and led her down a light, misty tunnel where she could see herself at the end, lying on the little bed. She stood beside her bed and watched the gentle lady rise up the tunnel, gathering up the stray notes of the song as she went and seeming very sorry to leave her. When the light around her began to dim, Rocky pleaded, "Please tell me who the song is about?"

The white lady seemed to sigh, "You will learn of Him soon. I promise." The music faded completely, and the light narrowed to a mere ribbon. She had never felt such yearning. Suddenly the pain extinguished the light, and she lay shivering in the warm darkness.

As the night passed, the breeze stiffened to a wind, and thunder rumbled in the distance. Rocky heard the roar of The Fat Man's bike as he entered the park and listened to its progress as it rolled to the overgrown corner where she waited in the trailer. Though her arm demanded her attention like a tiger with its teeth in her arm, behind the pain she remembered the gossamer music and effer-vescent light. She knew it was real, and not part of the sickness. Her tortured nerves reached for the memory, like a talisman against pain.

The motorcycle stopped nearby, and Rocky heard Jamie's voice. She was with The Fat Man, but they didn't stay outside. The Fat Man came into the trailer to her bedside. He touched her head with his fingers.

"She's burnin' up. You gotta get her to the hospital."

"I think she'll be better if I get her something to eat and she can drink some water. Will you help me get her arm wrapped up? I have a towel here somewhere."

"No, Jamie. Even in this light I can tell ye that her arm is busted and with the fever, she's in bad shape. How long since she ate?"

"This morning," she answered as she thought of the candy.

"If she dies, yer goin' to jail, babe." He slipped his arm under Rocky's shoulders. "It ain't right to let her suffer like that and you tryin' to pretend she's okay. She ain't."

"You think she gonna die?" She seemed to challenge him, but Rocky could hear that she was also afraid. Rocky had no strength to reassure her. She tried to whisper, "I heard music . . . in a place full of light." But though her lips moved, there was no sound. Jamie didn't hear, and she swayed as she stood on the metal step where the air was fresher than inside the trailer. "Maybe if we give her some whiskey, she'll wake up a little." She sounded desperate.

"I'm not gonna die. I heard the music, and the people were all in white" This time there was a little voice to her words, and The Fat Man heard.

"Yer girl been to heaven, babe. You better git her to the hospital before she stays there for keeps."

"You think they'll put me in jail even if she don't die?" Jamie still hung back. The Fat Man gently laid Rocky's injured arm on her chest, slipped his arm under her knees and lifted her.

"She don't weigh nothin'. We both know you haven't been feedin' her and it'd serve you right if the cops did put you somewhere for a while." The fat man pushed through the doorway.

"How can she get to the hospital anyway? I'm givin' her some J.D. In the old days they used it for medicine." Jamie produced a flask of whiskey and tipped it into Rocky's mouth before The Fat Man could turn away. Rocky gurgled and coughed. The liquid dribbled down her chin and soaked into her shirt.

"Stop it, Jamie! You're not gonna help her by dumpin' that in her mouth. It might get ya in worse trouble." Rocky smelled his beery breath mixed with body odor, but she moved her forehead against his soft neck where the beard didn't' grow. He didn't notice. Jamie slipped the flask into her waistband and followed him.

The Fat Man gave his light burden to Jamie as he climbed on the motorcycle. "Put her between us like a sandwich," he instructed, "and hold her arm against her chest to keep it still." Jamie leaned Rocky against his wide back with her arm wedged against him. Flames of pain shot through Rocky's elbow, into her shoulder and neck. When Jamie climbed on behind and put her arms around The Fat Man with Rocky in between, the intense pain gave her the feeling that she turned upside down like a cartwheel. The Fat Man jarred her again when he started the motorcycle.

"Go slow so she don't fall," Jamie said.

Lightening flashed and a deafening crash was simultaneous. It startled Jamie into squeezing a little more, and Rocky slipped into a faint that the pelting rain did not disturb.

Chapter 2

The Hospital

Rocky woke slowly, confused by the strange smells and sounds. The smooth bedrails gleamed in the morning light. One arm had a tube taped to it, and the other was splinted and bound with an elastic bandage. There was a man sweeping the floor near the bed.

"Am I kidnapped?"

The man laughed. "No honey, you're not kidnapped. You've been real sick, lying in that hospital bed for two days. I'll call a nurse to tell her that you woke up." He pushed the button near her ear.

The nurse was wearing pants and a shirt that looked like pajamas. "Hi, Rocky. We thought we were going to lose you for a while there. Can you drink a little water?"

"Where's my Mom?"

"She isn't here, honey. She brought you here so that we could help you. You were so sick that she was afraid that you'd die. If you know your phone number, you can call her up to let her know that you're going to be okay."

"We don't have a phone."

"Do you know your address? I would be happy to write her a letter to let her know."

Rocky's face brightened. "I live at 679 Evergreen Parkway, #19. It's a trailer place."

The nurse wrote the address on a pad from her pocket. "Oh, I didn't tell you that my name's Abby. I'm going to take care of you today. The first thing that we need to do is get you to start sipping some liquid. We'll start with water, then you get to choose your favorite juice. What kind would you like?"

Rocky looked sideways at the nurse. "Whatever you want to give me."

"Do you like apple juice?"

Rocky shrugged. The nurse brought some apple juice in a box with a tiny straw sticking out of the top. Rocky wished she hadn't put the straw in. It was easier to carry home to share with Jamie without any holes.

The next day a man about Jamie's age pushed her bed to a different room. He took everything off her sore arm and said he was going to take an X-ray of her bones. He turned her arm on its side and she yelped. "I'm sorry. I know it hurts, but before we can fix it, we need to see exactly what's wrong with it." He turned the arm again, and Rocky fainted.

The x-ray man put something that smelled like the bottles she picked up on Saturday morning under her nose, and she woke up. "I guess we'll have to get those pictures another way," he said as he went away.

A little later, a man with a mask over his nose and mouth gave her something to smell that he said smelled like bubble gum. Suddenly, she woke up back in her room. There was a cast on her arm like she had seen on a third grader at school. A man in green pajamas said that her arm wouldn't hurt as much with the cast on. He said his name was Doctor Ironwood. His breath smelled like coffee, and his hair was messy. Rocky wondered if he lived at the hospital all the time. His face was shaved smooth like Grandma's minister.

"Do you think you can eat some soup?" he asked. We want to get a little meat on your bones. I had the soup for lunch, and it was very good. It had lots of noodles."

She eyed him without turning her head toward him. He watched her for a moment and then wrote something on a paper on a clipboard and went into the hall. He said something to Abby, and a few minutes later, she brought Rocky a bowl of noodle soup. It tasted good.

"Does that man live here?"

"You mean the doctor? No, he goes home when he's done working."

"Why does he wear pajamas?"

"Those are called scrubs. It's so he won't get his regular clothes dirty, and scrubs are very comfortable. Sometimes he does have to stay here for a long time, if there aren't enough doctors to take care of everyone."

Rocky didn't think she could sleep if that man came in her room. She decided to stay awake until Abby told her he had gone home. But after she ate some of her soup and some crackers, Abby gave her some medicine, and she went to sleep in spite of herself.

The days in the hospital were a blur of fear and pain. As she grew stronger, she was more anxious to check on Jamie. She knew her mother couldn't get along without her help, and she vaguely remembered The Fat Man's threat that she would have to go to jail. She knew she had already been away much longer than ever before, even when she went to stay with Grandma.

It might have been two weeks since she woke in the hospital when Abby introduced her to a lady named Miss Charlene who said she was trying to find her mother, but was having a hard time. "You lived in a little trailer park down near a creek?" she asked.

Rocky nodded. "I live in the smallest trailer, in the part where the weeds are tall. I gave Abby my address. The Fat Man is in charge of it."

Miss Charlene read her address, and Rocky nodded.

"The address she gave us was evidently correct," Miss Charlene told Abby as she shook her head.

"Is Jamie kidnapped?" She hardly dared form the question.

Miss Charlene answered, "No, Rocky. We think that she went somewhere that she felt safer, but we don't know where that is. We'll keep trying to find out, and you don't need to worry."

"I think she went to Grandma's apartment to get some food and to tell Grandma to come help us. Her name is Carol because she was born on Christmas day."

"That's really good to know, and that will be a big help. That's neat that your grandmother's named for a Christmas Carol. I have a friend named Carol, but I don't think she's named that because she was born on a special day."

Rocky looked a little mystified, as she had never made the connection between her grandmother's name and birthday. She had simply heard her grandmother introduce herself to people with that information. She had always laughed when she said it.

We'll try to find your grandmother, honey, and we can check all the shelters, too. Had you been in the trailer long, Rocky?"

"We moved there when I was five. It's the smallest one with tall grass all around."

"Yes, I think I'm checking in the right place, and the trailer is empty. But I'll keep looking, and you don't need to worry."

"You need to ask The Fat Man. He's in charge of the park, and he's friends with my mom. He brought me here."

"Don't worry, Rocky. We'll take good care of you." Miss Charlene moved out into the hall with Abby, and Rocky saw them stop near her door and glance back at her as though they wanted to say something she couldn't hear.

Rocky quickly pulled the curtain around her bed and crept near the door out of view of the window. She heard Abby say that she needed to be in the hospital for two more weeks. She asked about the house where Rocky lived. Miss Charlene said that it was so tiny, that she half expected a hamster wheel on the inside but even the condition of the home would be grounds for child neglect and endangerment.

Rocky slipped back to her bed and sat on the side, thinking. She knew Jamie was afraid to be arrested. So if she couldn't go back to the trailer, she would go to Grandma's. She remembered that Grandma said she was sick, the last time she saw her. She didn't seem sick. It was easy for that lady to tell her not to worry, but Jamie needed her because they took care of each other.

During school days, Rocky got her lunch free in the cafeteria, and always got some extra or saved part of her lunch in her pocket. She found a plastic baggie with a zipper in the cafeteria trash can and used it so that nothing would stain her pocket. Sometimes the food Rocky brought her was the only thing she ate in the day. During the summer, Jamie brought home eggs and peanuts in her purse and took her to get samples at the grocery store. Rocky often found food in the trash cans around the park, but she didn't usually share that because her mother said she wouldn't eat garbage.

As Rocky considered, it seemed like it must be almost

time for school to start, and Jamie would be very hungry. Jamie used to wait in front of the trailer for her to come home, eager to see what she had in her pocket or backpack. *She might be waiting for me now, hoping I'll bring her something, and I can't get to her!* she thought. She squeezed her eyes very tightly so the tears couldn't come out. Even though everyone at the hospital said she wasn't kidnapped, they wouldn't let her leave and the lady at school had told the children that was what "kidnapped" meant. She was also angry that the lady said Jamie was gone. *She just wasn't looking in the right place!*

Rocky went to the bathroom and washed her face with a washcloth in cold water. *Jamie wouldn't let them find her and put her in jail.* But, she thought, *if her little girl came home, pretty soon Jamie would come back.* Abby startled her when she knocked on the bathroom door. "Rocky, your lunch is here."

When it seemed the nurse had left, she quickly retrieved the clothes she had come in. It was difficult to dress with her awkward cast, but when she had finished, she hurried to the tray where her lunch waited. She wrapped the roll and butter in the plastic that held her spoon and napkin. She emptied a pillowcase and dropped the food in. A piece of chicken breast was poised to follow when Abby spoke.

"Whatcha doin'? Goin' campin'?" Rocky jumped and

stared dumbly at the chicken in her hand. Abby took the pillow case from her gently and slid the roll and butter back onto the plate. She lifted Rocky up onto the bed and sat beside her.

"Sweetheart, I know you miss your mom. But, honey, Miss Charlene is looking everywhere, trying to find where she went. Miss Charlene has a car and a map, so it's much easier for her to find Mama Jamie than it would be for a little girl, all alone with no car. You don't have a car, do you?"

The child shook her head.

"If Miss Charlene finds Mama Jamie, she'll come here to tell you. So if you leave, then you'll be lost, and we'll have to hunt for Rocky! Will you stay here so that we can help you get stronger and so Miss Charlene will know where to find you?"

Rocky didn't know if she should promise or not. Jamie would know to stay away when she saw Miss Charlene's car, but she might get worried and come to the hospital looking for her. Finally she nodded without looking at Abby.

"You can stay dressed if you want to. Your clothes are much nicer than these funny old hospital gowns."

Rocky forced herself to swallow under Abby's careful watch, even though her throat was tight and she felt like she was eating Jamie's food. Every day, the hospital gave her enough food for three days and it was good food too. If only Jamie would come and sit on her bed, and they could enjoy it together.

She also wanted to tell her what had happened to her the night she broke her arm. Jamie would like to hear about the place that was filled with clean, smiling people dressed in white. But she wanted, more than anything, to tell her about the inexpressibly beautiful music. She knew that if Jamie could hear the music, everything would be different.

❧ ❧ ❧

The little girl was strong enough to leave after four weeks. Miss Charlene helped her dress in new clothes. They were much nicer than what she had before, and the little pink sandals fit perfectly.

"I'm going to look pretty for my mom!" Rocky said. "I've wished she'd come see me in the hospital so much, but finally I can see her!"

Miss Charlene kneeled down in front of the child. "Rocky, I still haven't been able to find your mama. I went to the address you gave me, but nobody was there. And now the trailer is gone too. The park manager said that nobody had paid anything for the spot for a long time, and the toilet was overflowing. The neighbors complained about the odor so much that the manager had the city come take it away.

Rocky was dubious that Charlene really knew the right place to look, but still her mind raced to another explanation. *She might have had an accident and be hurt somewhere! When she gets well, she'll come back to get me,* she thought. *But how will she know where to find me?*

Suddenly, Rocky screamed. "I want to go home! You have to take me home! You can't kidnap me. I'll scream and yell until the cops come and put *you* in jail!"

Miss Charlene bit her lip. "Honey, I'm so sorry that we can't find your mama. We think we found your grandma, but she's in a hospital and is too sick to help. Her doctors are trying to help her, but they don't know if she'll get well." The concern on Miss Charlene's face confused Rocky.

"I thought you said I got to go home today."

"Your old home isn't there anymore."

Rocky wiped the tears from her cheeks fiercely. "You're a liar!"

"I know you feel very sad about your mom and grandma. Did you know that it is my job to help you be safe and to try to find your mom? If I had any idea where else to look, I would. But for now I don't have any clues."

Rocky's defiance melted away and fear huddled in her

brown eyes. "Where are you taking me?" she whispered.

"There is a nice lady I know who is waiting to meet you. Her name is Mrs. Duffin. She and Mr. Duffin are what are called "foster parents." They want to take care of you. If we can find your Mom, then we will do whatever we feel was best for you and her. Would you like to meet Mrs. Duffin?

Rocky hesitated, but finally nodded. Charlene called Mrs. Duffin in from the hall. The lady that entered was slender with soft, gray eyes. She was wearing jeans and a light-pink tee-shirt. Her voice was as sweet as a child's.

"Hello, Rocky, I'm Lillian Duffin. I hope I'm going to get to be your foster mom." She put out her hand, but Rocky only looked at it. Mrs. Duffin lifted Rocky's hand and squeezed gently. "I have a pretty bedroom waiting for you at my house. It has carpet on the floor and a pink bed cover and white curtains. I also have a swing-set in my backyard. Would you like to come and see them?"

Rocky stared at Mrs. Duffin then shook her head. She turned to Miss Charlene and begged, "Will you take me to my home so I can look for my mother?"

"Yes, Rocky, I'll take you by there. Then we'll go over to see the Duffin's house. There are four children already, and they're looking forward to meeting you too. You'll meet Mr. Duffin later on, because he is at work right now and couldn't come."

"Will you let me stay with my mom if we find her? I know I can find her if you'll drive me there."

Mrs. Duffin knelt down in front of Rocky. "If you find your mom, we'll have her come over to our house too. Do you have any favorite food that we can have for your welcome dinner? We want you to know how happy we are to have you come."

Rocky glanced into Mrs. Duffin's face and then at her feet. "I don't like sour milk," she said.

"We'll make sure that the milk isn't sour. Anything else?"

"I like the school spaghetti."

"I like the school spaghetti too! I think I can make some like that. I'll see you after a little while. Okay?"

"If I don't find my mother today, I'll come over with Miss Charlene."

"That's good." Mrs. Duffin smiled

❧ ❧ ❧

Charlene Hollister cringed inwardly as Rocky became excited when her car turned into the trailer park. "This is the right place! Go this way and then to the end!" The child pointed. The car rolled past the dilapidated trailer homes. Rocky strained forward as the big tree came into view, and then she gasped. The little clearing where the travel trailer had been was empty. She stared hard as though it would appear by magic if her eyes were keen enough. When Miss Charlene stopped the car, Rocky jumped out and ran to the empty space searching the deep grass. "I *know* this is the right place. I can smell the pee."

The little girl looked into the large tree as though the trailer might have magically ascended it.

"Mama!" she screamed suddenly. "Jamie, it's me, Rocky, home from the hospital!" She waited. The social worker watched Rocky's shoulders rise and fall as sobs heaved them and were fought down again. She steeled her heart against the pain swelling there for the pathetic little creature calling into the heavens and waiting for an answer her professional experience told her would never come.

The little blonde girl turned slowly around and around, searching with wonder and confusion and pain blended in her features. Her face brightened a little, and she came over to Charlene. "One time Grandma took me to the library, and I watched a movie where a tornado picked up a house with a girl in it and put it down in a magical land called Oz. Do you think that might have happened to Jamie?"

Charlene was a well-trained, experienced social worker, and she knew that it was better not to deceive the child. “I don’t think so,” she said softly. Rocky became businesslike. She got into the car and shut the door while Charlene still stood outside.

“I need to talk to The Fat Man” Rocky spoke through the open window.

“Where is he? Do you mean the park manager?”

“By the little sign that says “office.” I’ll show you where to stop. You *said* you talked to him.”

The car stopped near the gate that hung crooked by a broken hinge. A big motorcycle was parked in the weedy, chain-link yard. Rocky pushed past a ragged screendoor and rang a doorbell mounted on a narrow counter. She held it down until The Fat Man emerged through a dark doorway. Mild surprise registered in his shaggy face when he saw Rocky. She ran to him and threw her arms around his legs as he watched Miss Charlene with narrowed eyes.

“Rocky wanted to talk to you; she’s looking for her mother.”

“I dunno where yer mom is, Rocky,” he said. “She disappeared after the night we dropped you off.”

Charlene’s attention sharpened. “You dropped Rocky off at the hospital?”

“Yeah, me and Jamie saw that she was real sick. We

brung her on the Harley."

"Are you Rocky's father?"

"Noooooo way! I only met Jamie two years ago. We were in a drinkin' party, and she had a little trailer. I let her park it in the clearing at the end of the lane there, even though there ain't no hookups. She usually got her mom to come dump for her, and bring food and such, but she dint come for a long while and it got bad. After we took the little girl to the hospital . . ."

Rocky interrupted, "Did you see the white people and hear the music when you took me on the motorcycle?"

A strange look passed through The Fat Man's eyes, but he shook his head. "You was delirious. I could see that you was real sick so I helped your mama get you to the hospital." Rocky frowned, but The Fat Man continued his narrative peeling the girl's arms from around his legs. "I took Jamie to her mom's. The mom was gone, and the neighbor said she was in the hospital. Jamie busted into the place and got the mom's keys to the truck. Then she gave me this."

The Fat Man reached under the counter and handed Miss Charlene a sealed envelope addressed to Rocky. Miss Charlene turned it over to break the seal. Rocky noticed her name and snatched it from her. She ran outside to a corner of the yard where the grass was higher than her shoulder and sank down. The dirty envelope held a sheet of folded notebook paper.

Dear Rocky,

If you get this letter, you know that I'm gone. I cant take care of you anymore. Grama has bad cancer and cant get us food and other stuf. Im not a good mom, and shood have took beter care of you. I hope you will grow up and be happy and dont take to the booze like I did. The booze ruint my life and even thogh I want to be a good mom, the cops will put me in jail if they find out it was me let you starve. I do love you, and hope you dont forgit me, only dont rember that I dint take good care of you. the fat man sez the social servise will find a home for you, wher they dont drink or do drugs. so I hope you have a good house and your new mom takes good care of you. Don't let nobody hurt you.

Love Jamie"

Hot tears ran down the hollow cheeks. Rocky held the paper to her face, hoping to smell a trace of her mother's scent. The paper tasted salty when she licked it. She kissed the writing and folded it carefully. She put it under her shirt and held it against her heaving chest. At last she stood up and walked to where Miss Charlene waited. The Fat Man returned to his den.

"Jamie's not here." The words were brusque.

"Does the letter tell you where to find her?"

"No. It says don't forget her. It says she was not a good mom. It says she will come and get me when she can." The child's fortitude melted away, and she covered her face with her hands and sobbed. Miss Charlene picked her up, and Rocky nestled her cheek on the soft shoulder. For a moment she imagined that she was on Jamie's shoulder. Then her body stiffened, and the social worker set her gently on the seat. The car window reflected her lowered brow and clenched teeth.

Chapter 3

The Duffins

Lillian Duffin felt her stomach lurch when Charlene Hollister's car stopped at the curb. She suddenly remembered the first time she swam in the ocean. She hated the way the moving water brushed unknown things against her legs. She didn't want to step where she could not see, and the powerful tide pulled her small body irresistibly. Her brothers laughed at her and swam under the green water and grabbed her legs. She had shrieked in terror. That only encouraged them, and they continued their teasing. At last, she retreated to the sand and spent the day collecting shells.

Now she tried to remember why she and Brian had decided to take a foster child. It seemed like a vast, unknown step into dangerous water.

She stopped the gentle rocking of the porch swing and slid her youngest daughter off her lap. Though it was cool on the covered porch, Lillian suddenly felt sweaty. She planted her steps firmly on the cement and met Rocky and Charlene on the walk.

"Welcome, Rocky! We've been waiting for you on the porch. This is my youngest daughter, Amber. She just had her fifth birthday."

"I'm seven." Rocky said it with a distinct air of superiority. She marched ahead of the others into the house and looked around. The rooms were neat and the furnishings pretty. There were flowers in vases in every room, and their perfume wafted in the cool air.

"Air conditioning." Rocky said.

"Amber, why don't you show Rocky where her room is?" Mrs. Duffin suggested.

Amber peeked out from behind her mother's hip at the newcomer. The girls were almost the same size, with Amber having a slight edge. She slipped her hand into Rocky's, but the older girl snatched back her hand.

Amber was effectively rebuffed, but her mother whispered, "She's not ready to hold your hand. Just let her follow you." The two girls trailed out of the room, a scowl on the older girl's face.

"I take it she didn't find what she was expecting to find," Lillian said.

"Right. I took her by the trailer park where she had lived, and she saw for herself that the trailer that she had lived in was gone. She went out into the clearing where it had been and called "Jamie! Jamie!" and then just stood there waiting. I don't think I'll ever get to the point when those types of scenes don't wrench my heart. I hope I don't. She told me she had seen a movie about a house and a girl flying to a place called Oz and wondered if her mother might have gone there. When I told her no, she seemed to begin forming some other ideas, and said she needed to talk to The Fat Man." Lillian Duffin raised her eyebrows, waiting for an explanation.

"Well, I hoped that maybe he was her father, but I don't think he is. He's the park manager, and Rocky didn't know his real name. He had a letter from Jamie to Rocky. I didn't get to read it, because she grabbed it out of my hand and ran away with it. I could see that it was a page of handwriting, but Rocky folded it up into its envelope and put it into the waistband of her shorts next to her skin. I really do need to know what's in it, because if it's a 'goodbye' letter, it would allow us to terminate parental rights more quickly. My gut tells me the mother is gone for good. She was devastated when she read it."

"She can read?"

"Yes, the nurses in the hospital said that she reads quite well for a seven-year-old. Her school records also show her to be an exceptionally bright child. By the way, we found her birth records, and her legal name is Roxanne Leila Davis."

"What a pretty name. It's hard to imagine that her mother would name her like that and then call her 'Rocky'."

"Well, maybe she wanted a tough sounding nickname to make her less vulnerable. Her fear of men is still very strong, and she would never speak to the male doctors or orderlies. But there's no doubt that she's a bright child. If we give her half a chance, I think she'll do very well. At any rate, if you can get the letter from her, photocopy it and return it to her without her knowing that it's been bothered, I think that would be the best."

"Is there any other suggestion you can give us for reaching her?" Lillian's voice had a desperate edge. "Do you know *anything* else?"

"Well, she seems to be well-attached to her mother, and so much of what she is dealing with is plain grief. She was starved and filthy, but her broken arm was a new injury, and there don't seem to be any old breaks. She said she broke her arm when she fell out of a tree when she was too sick to hold on. The doctors think it was true from the appearance of the swelling and x-ray. She has no physical sign of being otherwise molested, but we can't be totally sure. Her school teachers suspected sexual abuse because she was so afraid of men, but the current evidence indicates only severe neglect. She was sometimes quite friendly in the hospital and seemed astonished that her mother would leave her. I think that if she is encouraged to talk about her mom, and hopefully to go through the mourning process, she can heal."

"Poor little angel" Lillian said.

"Yes, poor little angel, but I know that your loving home will be good for her if any will. I think you'll find your way into her wounded little heart and help it heal." Charlene heaved a sigh. "I have to run. I have a court appointment downtown in an hour. Good luck."

Lillian watched as the social worker pulled away from the curb. Then she bowed her head and sent up a prayer without formed words, but that contained all the doubt and fear of the strange, new child and sorrow for the suffering she endured.

Lillian opened her eyes and was startled that the two little girls were watching her from the doorway.

"Were you praying?" Amber asked.

"You caught me! I was praying that Rocky would be happy in our family." Rocky stuck out her chin in silent defiance.

Chapter 4

Dinner

The little newcomer sat rigid in the chair assigned to her. She could feel the eyes of the older boy and two girls watching her. The man that had been introduced as Mr. Duffin seemed huge from his seat at the head of the table. Mrs. Duffin was smaller than Jamie. She hardly looked older than the big boy who sat beside her. The man was gray at the temples, clean-shaven with clear blue eyes. He smiled at Rocky and knelt down to shake her hand when he came in, but the hand he lifted was trembling. He was tall like the man in the yellow car, and he smelled like the x-ray man in the hospital that had twisted her broken arm. Now, as she stared straight ahead, the crowd of seven around the table seemed like many more than that to the foster child. She sat between Amber and Mrs. Duffin and wished that they were not so close. She had never sat at a table for a meal inside a home before. Even at Grandma's they ate on the couch in front of the TV.

There were several dishes of food on the table and a big jug of milk. Mr. Duffin asked Josh to "say the blessing." Amber whispered in Rocky's ear to fold her arms for the prayer but Rocky continued to stare at the opposite wall. Mr. Duffin told Josh to "go ahead."

"Do you like spaghetti, Rocky?" Mr. Duffin's voice boomed from his end of the table. Rocky swallowed and shook her head. Mrs. Duffin had already served a small pile onto her plate, and turned to her when she responded negatively.

"You told me that you liked spaghetti! I hoped that it was one of your favorites." Rocky shook her head again. Mrs. Duffin seemed a bit miffed but served some bread, jam and broccoli onto her plate. She poured milk into her glass, and Rocky changed her staring to the filled glass until the others seemed to have shifted their attention to their dinners. She glanced at Mr. Duffin and then to Josh. The boy took very big bites and sucked the noodles into his mouth with a slurpy noise. He had a napkin tucked into the neck of his shirt and used it to wipe his chin after almost every bite. He had enough spaghetti on his plate for three meals for Rocky and Jamie.

One of the older girls asked Rocky if she liked her new bedroom. Rocky was silent.

"Rocky needs some time to get used to us and this new place." Mrs. Duffin answered for her. "Have you ever seen such a big family before?"

"No." The newcomer answered at last. "Why do you have so many kids?"

"Because we don't have to take our turn doing the dishes or mowing the lawn as often with more people," Mr. Duffin joked. The little girl turned only her eyes when he spoke, but wondered if they wanted her to work for them.

The chocolate pudding with whipped cream was served and eaten before Rocky had tasted anything. At last Mrs. Duffin got up and whispered something to Mr. Duffin. He nodded.

"Josh, Katy, Kristen, you three come outside with me. I want you to help me in the garden for a few minutes." He stifled the rising complaints with a quick glance at the untouched plate, and they each picked up their own dishes and left the room without further comment.

Mrs. Duffin began to clear the empty dishes and put away leftovers. Amber continued beside Rocky, eating her pudding in pea-sized bites. When Mrs. Duffin was out of the room, Rocky seized her glass of milk and drank it without a breath. She grabbed her spoon and shoveled the awkward spaghetti into her mouth. The broccoli and bread disappeared into her pocket, and then she wolfed down the pudding, keeping her eye on the door to the kitchen. When Mrs. Duffin returned Rocky wiped her mouth with her napkin the way the boy had done and stared straight ahead, hoping Mrs. Duffin wouldn't scold her. But Amber's mouth hung open in amazement, and she pointed when she said, "She put the bread and broccoli in her pocket!"

"It's okay. She needs to get used to us, and that may take a little while.

"May I go?" Rocky was unable to cover the faint tremor in her voice.

"Sure, Rocky. Put your dirty dishes in the sink in the kitchen, and then you're all done. It's Amber's and my turn to do the dishes tonight, but I'll teach you how to do them too when your turn comes. Your partner in doing dishes is going to be Katy."

As Rocky hurried upstairs, she heard Amber retelling how she had eaten her dinner with some exaggerations. She rushed into the pretty little room and shut the door to shield herself from the sound of their voices. She was ashamed of herself. She knew Mrs. Duffin would think she had very bad manners. But she was so hungry, and it seemed impossible to eat with so many people watching her. She took the bread and broccoli out of her pocket and hid them in the bottom of her pillow case. Since they had taken away the food she had saved in the hospital, she decided to hide it where she could guard it even in her sleep. Hopefully she'd find a way to get it to Jamie before it got too old and dry. She was careful to keep it away from the letter that was also hidden there.

The window in the small room overlooked the back yard. She saw Mr. Duffin and the older children digging weeds in the garden. Mr. Duffin swung the hoe, and it cut deep into the dirt. He picked up the big weed he had unearthed and flung it into the trash can at the corner of the garden. Rocky saw his muscles working through his shirt and the dark sweat stain that was growing larger on his back. Even from her high vantage point, he seemed huge. Echo's of warnings reverberated in her mind in Jamie's voice. "Men will hurt you if they can. Never give them a chance!" She shivered and hugged herself. Jamie was gone away the nights when the man with the yellow car tried to come into their trailer. She wished she had been better at keeping him from hurting her.

Despite the associations, she was curious and wanted to see what they were doing and listen to what they said about her. She braced herself against the wall and shoved the dresser in front of the door to her room. It wasn't too heavy, since she didn't have much in it, but she moved very carefully so it wouldn't make noise or bump on the door handle.

Rocky heard the backdoor slam and returned to her window vantage point. Mrs. Duffin dried her hands on a dish towel as she picked her way over toys toward her husband. She leaned on the garden gate and looked up into his face. Rocky thought she looked like a child with her head tipped back that way. He seemed concerned by what his wife was saying. He slipped his glove off and laid a hand lightly on her shoulder. He said something Rocky could not distinguish, and then kissed his wife lightly on the lips. She patted his shoulder three times as he slipped his glove on and turned back to hoeing. Mrs. Duffin watched for a minute and then flipped the dish-towel toward his backside so it made a pop. He turned and grinned at her, and turned back to his work again.

Mrs. Duffin called Josh to do the dishes, then waved at her daughters. When she caught their attention, she gestured toward her husband's bent back and they nodded. Josh had to lean down to drape his arm around his mother's neck as they walked to the house. Kristin was watering the bushes with a hose, and Katy had a watering can. Suddenly they both turned their streams of water on Mr. Duffin. Rocky heard him roar as the cold water soaked him. He grabbed the garbage can lid, and using it as a shield, overtook the hose, and pulled it out of

Kristin's hands. He turned it on her and followed her as she ran into the back porch. When she opened the door, Rocky could hear both of them laughing. Katy had used their distraction to run and turn off the water tap. As Mr. Duffin ran to turn it on, she ran into the house and locked the door. Mr. Duffin soon discovered that he was exiled, and he sprayed the windows where his laughing daughters watched him. Rocky heard someone running up the stairs and into the bathroom next to her room. The window squeaked as it opened and suddenly a shower of water poured down on Mr. Duffin. Rocky heard Mrs. Duffin laugh wickedly when Mr. Duffin raised his astonished face.

"*Et tu, Brute*?" he yelled. A big blue towel fluttered out of the upstairs window.

"That won't earn you forgiveness!" he yelled at the upstairs window. "I know where you sleep!" Another cascade of water came down wetting the towel he had draped on his head. Suddenly he squirted into the open bathroom window, and Mrs. Duffin slammed it shut with a squeal. Rocky rushed from the window to the bed as Mrs. Duffin ran past her door. Lillian must have heard her scamper and tapped the door. When Rocky didn't answer, Lillian tried to come in, but she could open it only enough to see that the dresser was in the way.

"Honey, move the dresser back where it goes. You don't need to block the door." Rocky obeyed her and sat on the bed as she waited for Lillian to come in. She was surprised that Mrs. Duffin was smiling when she did. “We are having a water fight. He always starts it, and so we decided to gang up on him to pay him back. We’re only playing.”

Rocky remembered a time when Jamie took her for a walk in a summer rainstorm. They had splashed in the puddles and squished their bare toes in the mud. Jamie carried her home when she got chilly and dried her with a blue towel. Rocky’s attention jerked back to the stranger who smiled down at her and her face crumpled into tears.

Lillian sat on the bed beside the sobbing child. "Are you thinking about your mother?”

She nodded slightly, but otherwise ignored the adult until Lillian slipped out of the room and shut the door behind her.

A little later, two new story books slid under the door. One was Cinderella and the other was about a mouse that got lost. Rocky read them both and then read them again. Cinderella had a mean new family but ended up happy with the prince. The mouse rode in a bicycle basket and jumped out when he saw his house. She returned to the window and confirmed that a pink bicycle leaned against the fence in the back yard. She must learn to ride it, she thought.

At bedtime, Amber showed Rocky a drawer where

there were new panties and two new nightgowns trimmed with pretty lace. There were other clothes in the dresser, but Rocky didn't unfold them. They weren't like her own clothes.

She slid the pink nighty over her head while studying herself in the mirror. *I look like a girl in a magazine*, she thought. She remembered cutting out pictures of girls in expensive clothes from the Sunday fliers that came in the neighbor's newspapers. She used the glue stick from her school bag to stick them in her spiral notebook. When she had all the best ones done, she woke Jamie, and they decided which ones were prettiest. The fact that Jamie always chose brown-eyed blondes regardless of the clothes was not lost on Rocky. Once she had even said, "She looks most like you. She's the prettiest."

Now Rocky had the fancy clothes, but Jamie was not there to admire her. She felt as flat as a paper doll.

Amber showed her a new toothbrush and began to show her how to brush her teeth.

"I can brush my own teeth!" Rocky snapped. Amber watched and saw that she *did* do it right, but she didn't use toothpaste and the bristles of the toothbrush were bloodstained. Lillian showed her how much toothpaste she should use, and Rocky tried it. It tasted good, but when she swallowed it, Amber corrected her. 'It will make your teeth look bad if you swallow it. You're supposed to spit it out." She spit a little in the sink and wearily curled up on top of the bedspread.

Amber started to explain that she should crawl under the covers. Rocky shrugged, as though she had known, but chose not to comply. Amber stood by the bed, looking at her. At last Rocky opened her eyes and growled at Amber, "Don't stare at me!"

Amber's gaze remained steady. She said, "My mother says that you miss your mom and feel lonely."

Rocky glared unblinking. Amber tiptoed to her adjacent bedroom and padded back with something cradled in her arms. The old cloth doll she held had once been pretty but was now tattered from loving.

"This is my Molly Dolly, who I always sleep with. She helps me not be afraid, and when Mama sends me to my room for time out, I hug her and kiss her and she makes me feel better. You can sleep with her tonight to help you feel better."

Rocky didn't move, so Amber hesitantly laid the little dolly in the curve of Rocky's body. Rocky grabbed the doll's arm and threw her to the floor. She swung her legs over the side of the bed and stomped on the dolly's face. Amber snatched the doll with a cry and held her against her shoulder. "Don't you ever stomp on Molly again! You're a brat! You're mean! Molly didn't want to stay in here with a meany, but I told her she should." One stormy glare met another until Amber fled to her mother's arms. Rocky smiled a flat, pretty, paper-doll smile.

❧ ❧ ❧

In the night, muffled sobbing woke Amber. She knew that Rocky was awake, and she slipped out of her covers with Molly under her arm. She stood in the doorway of the darkened room and watched. Grief had never touched her short life, and she couldn't understand the power of such pain. Nevertheless, her heart was softened toward the persecutor of her little doll. She thought of what it would be like if *her* mother disappeared when she was sick and tears started in her own eyes. She struggled against her impulse, but at last rushed to the bed and threw her arms around Rocky. The older girl didn't push her away and allowed her solo sobbing to become a duet. Rocky held something paper that crackled as Amber hugged her.

The two little girls wept together until Rocky was able to swallow her sobs. Amber pulled two tissues from the bedside box and shared one with her foster sister. Rocky's expression chilled suddenly and she grew silent, like the dropping of a curtain on a stage. The younger girl slid off the bed, paused for a moment and then thrust Molly into the other's arms. She squared her shoulders and left the room without looking back.

Mr. and Mrs. Duffin talked into the morning hours,

wondering if they had been rash in accepting the placement. 'It's all new to her," Brian reassured his wife. She can't enjoy anything until she's used to us and to our house. She'll succumb to your kindness and my charm soon enough." Lillian couldn't relax enough to believe him.

"You're always the optimist. What if she never can let us get close enough to help her?"

"In a year, we'll not be able to imagine our family without Rocky. We need to get used to her, too. We're seeing the very worst, but pretty soon, we'll see her gifts, too."

"What if we're only seeing the tip of the iceberg? What if she's not safe for our other children?"

"She's only seven. You have enough experience with seven-year-olds and enough extra training to help civilize and teach an orangutan. Go to sleep and see if tomorrow isn't a much better day."

Lillian lay still until her husband's breathing became deep and even and then began to snore softly. She slipped out of bed and wrapped herself in a cotton bathrobe. She paced while her imagination exaggerated the worst possibilities into frightening extremes. At last, she tip-toed into the bedroom where the child slept.

Something lay on the foot of the bed, and she had to

come close to see that Rocky's extra pillow cushioned Molly Dolly's head. She knew Amber had helped her in a weeping fest, but smiled to see that she had risked the little doll a second time. Amber didn't make sacrifices easily, and Lillian smiled a little. As the light strengthened, she noticed that Rocky clutched a crumpled envelope under her cheek.

Chapter 5

Braiding

"Rocky, wake up!" For a moment Rocky believed Jamie was shaking her. She smiled and reached out to her as she opened her eyes. Amber saw the smile, but the stony mask that had guarded the inner wounds for several weeks at the Duffins quickly replaced it with a faint whimper.

Amber drew back and stated, "You have to get up and get ready to go school shopping." The little bridge formed between the two girls on the first night was fragile and neither had crossed it often since. But this morning, Amber's delight at the prospect of shopping overwhelmed her reserve, and she skipped toward the door. "I'm going to kindergarten, and I need my own backpack!" she chimed in a sing-song voice. She turned back to the little girl sitting in the bed. "You get a new backpack too, and new shoes and clothes!"

Shopping! Rocky thought. She had been on several watchful grocery excursions with Mrs. Duffin, but the Duffins went to different stores than Jamie did. She had never even seen a familiar street or business since she came, but she hadn't been shopping for clothes. Surely Mrs. Duffin would like to find good deals at the thrift store like Grandma did, and it seemed like anything familiar would lead her to Jamie. *If I see her*, the child thought, *Mrs. Duffin will let her help me find good deals.* She extended that idea to conclude, *Mrs. Duffin would bring Jamie home and feed her and let her get cleaned up as Grandma used to.* She didn't hope that they could return to the trailer anymore, but she knew that Grandma would let them come to her house.

She pulled on the clothes she had been wearing when she went to the hospital. She wanted Jamie to recognize her. The more she thought about it, the more certain it seemed that this would be a very good day. She ran to the bathroom after hastily dropping her nightgown into her drawer. She scrubbed her face and hands and smiled at herself as she brushed her hair. Mrs. Duffin noticed her through the open door and stopped to observe.

"Today is the day we're going school shopping," Rocky informed her. Lillian smiled at her in the mirror, and Rocky did not withdraw from the eye contact.

She gathered her courage, "Will you do my hair in a fancy braid today? I can't do it very good with a cast."

Lillian dropped the laundry basket she was holding, spilling the clothes in her eagerness. "Of course, I'd love to!" She gathered the necessary equipment from the bathroom drawer and sat on the toilet lid. She pulled Rocky to her backward and began creating a complicated braid pattern. It was difficult, as Rocky repeatedly turned her head to see in the mirror, but Lillian chattered as she worked. "I'm so glad you let me braid your hair. It is so pretty, and I love to braid hair. My older girls won't grow their hair long enough, and Amber's hair is so fine that it falls out quickly."

"Jamie braids my hair sometimes for school. She does it so tight that it stays in all week."

"I don't think I can get it that tight, but I'll do my best," Lillian said.

I drink the sour milk," Rocky bragged. "It tastes terrible, but my Mom says it makes my hair pretty. I plug my nose and drink it."

Lillian performed a few more twists and then asked, "You told me when I first met you that you didn't like sour milk, but you drank the sour milk to get pretty hair?" Lillian failed in her attempt to keep her voice light and the little girl noticed the change.

"I drank the sour milk mostly because I was so hungry all the time. When I went to school, they would give me food for free, but in the summer, we had to get samples and find stuff in the park. Grandma used to bring us bags of food, but she might be sick, because she didn't bring us anything for a long time. Jamie said to drink the milk because the girls in the magazines drink it to get pretty hair. Did you know that the girls in the magazines get a million dollars for having their pictures taken? Jamie said I was pretty enough to be in the magazines, and sour milk works pretty good." She turned her head to get a side view of the braiding process.

"Yep, that sour milk must have done its job, because your hair is very pretty." Lillian brightened her tone with effort. "I think that once it gets so pretty, you don't need to have sour milk anymore to keep it that way. It just grows pretty from the roots from then on. Besides that, sweet milk will give you good strong bones and help your arm heal." The little girl didn't answer as Lillian finished her braiding. "All done. I think it's a pretty good job, don't you?"

Rocky nodded. It wasn't the way Jamie did it, but it

did look nice.

"Hurry and get dressed and come to breakfast. It's almost time to go shopping!" Lillian said with a gentle push.

Rocky turned to Lillian as she gathered the laundry back into the basket and whispered, "Mrs. Duffin? I *do* like your food."

"I know. You were just nervous when you first got here, weren't you? I'm so glad you have been so brave and are doing so well." The little girl brushed past her foster-mother, but there was a tiny hint of pleasure in her expression.

Chapter 5

Shopping

Mrs. Duffin parked in the crowded lot. The older children piled out, each one pausing to rehearse where and when they would meet their mother. They each had their school-clothing money and were excited at the prospect of the day's shopping. Rocky and Amber waited for Mrs. Duffin to lock the minivan, and then she held out her hands for the little girls to hold. Amber complied, but Rocky pretended not to see the offered hand. "Please hold my hand Rocky. I need to keep you safe with all these cars and people rushing around."

Rocky placed a limp hand on Mrs. Duffin's fingers, and the three of them hurried toward the big department store. It wasn't where Rocky had hoped to go. She had never seen this big store before, and she didn't think it was anywhere near her old trailer house. Suddenly, she noticed an old truck pulling a small travel trailer out on the boulevard. Delight raced through her. She studied the trailer and knew it was not hers, but the sight of it reminded her that she didn't know where Jamie had gone. *Maybe she lived near this store now!* She tightened her grip on Mrs. Duffin's hand and she studied the stores they approached with interest and touched her braids lightly.

She wondered what Jamie would do when she saw her. She felt sure she would notice her, looking as pretty as she did. Rocky thought she would run to her. *She might even pick me up like she used to do when I was little and kiss my cheeks. Jamie will tell Mrs. Duffin that she is my mother and will take care of me now. She'll explain that she's been searching everywhere for me and had finally come to this store in hope of seeing me. She'll say she had almost given up hope of ever finding her baby!* Rocky's heart raced as she searched for the familiar form that seemed, as Rocky's imagination grew more active, more certainly in the department store.

The shoe department was crowded with children and parents buying for school. Rocky insisted on walking up and down each aisle before settling down to make her choices near the rack that held her size. She looked and listened, but there was nothing that offered hope. She found some hot pink canvas shoes in the clearance bin that looked just like her shoes for last year. "I want these!" she stated. Mrs. Duffin tried to dissuade her, pointing out that there were much sturdier, nicer shoes, but the child would not be convinced. The girls-clothing department provided a similar scene. Rocky embraced shorts and shirts from the summer clearance rack. "I love these! I was worried that I couldn't find any, but I did after all!"

Only when Mrs. Duffin allowed her to put them in the shopping basket did Rocky consider warmer, dressier outfits.

Though they found several skirts and tops that fit well and Rocky liked, she caressed the summery flowered shirts almost continuously.

Amber found several skirt sets and two dresses to wear to school. She confided that her mom had told her that she could wear dresses every day to kindergarten if she wanted to, and she *was* going to. Her mother slipped in two pairs of jeans for each girl, but Rocky pulled the shorts sets out from underneath so that they remained on top of the pile.

When the trio moved on to where the backpacks were

displayed, Rocky's spirits sagged. Though Amber vacillated between two possible purchases, Rocky grabbed the first backpack she found and then stood at the end of the aisle watching the customers hurrying past. When Amber finally made up her mind, Rocky followed as they made their way to the check-out. She knew Mrs. Duffin would not want to tour each store in the mall searching for Jamie, but surely the trip would not be altogether fruitless.

Suddenly she rushed forward with a cry of joy. She threw her arms around the thighs of a young woman with straight untrimmed blonde hair who was waiting in a check-out line. She was wearing a tank shirt and tight jeans. She whirled around in amazement to see her assailant. Rocky drew back a little and looked joyfully up into the young woman's face. She jumped backward. "Oh!" she cried as though the woman had the face of a monster.

Lillian hurried forward. "Rocky?"

The child grabbed Mrs. Duffin's hand. "I thought it was Jamie," she mumbled.

"I'm sorry." Mrs. Duffin apologized to the bewildered customer. "She mistook you for someone she misses very much."

Lillian paid for their choices and hurried them to the car. She saw that the little girls were strapped in and slipped in a CD with soft music. Nobody spoke as they drove around the mall to the pizza parlor where the older kids were going to meet them. When they stopped, Lillian handed her a tissue, and Rocky blew her nose. Lillian helped Amber out of her seat and came around the car to bring Rocky, but the little girl stared out the window, like a single goldfish in a bowl, and made no attempt to get out. Lillian unfastened her, and Rocky let her take her hand. The arm with the cast hung down. "Maybe Jamie wouldn't recognize me with the cast anyway," she said.

Chapter 6

Concern

Lillian and Amber knelt beside Amber's bed for prayers. Amber watched with one eye open as Lillian settled herself and bowed her head. "Close your eyes, Mamma, so I can say prayers." Lillian obeyed with a hint of a smile.

"Dear Heavenly Father, I am thankful for my family and my home and for my kindergarten and for my teacher, Mrs. Jensen, and for my Church teacher (a pause). I can't remember her name, but she is Cammy's mom. I thank thee for my nice bed," another pause, and then she continued in a serious, quieter voice, "I thank thee that Rocky could come and live with us and be my sister, and I thank thee that she is good in her class."

Here Amber stopped, her brow furrowed. "Heavenly Father? Rocky is very sad about her Mom leaving her. She never wants to play, and she cries in her bed at night and I can hear her. It seems like all night long. Please help her to feel better so that she can be happy and have a good Christmas in seven weeks and three days. Help her not to be afraid of Dad and Josh anymore because they like her and want her to be happy, too. Please help me be good, too, and keep my room clean. Help Santa to remember that I want a new pink bike that doesn't have flat tires for Christmas. In the name of Jesus Christ, Amen."

"Will Heavenly Father answer my prayer, Mom?"

"I know that Heavenly Father always answers our prayers when we pray for something good that we need. He always wants us to pray for those that we love, because he loves them too." Lillian thought for a moment. "Sometimes He helps us to know what to do to make our prayers come true. He uses people to answer prayers. We need to watch and listen and think so that we can help Heavenly Father answer that prayer for Rocky."

Amber circled her mother's neck with her arms and looked into her eyes. "I love you, Mama."

"I love you too, honey."

Chapter 7

Dad's Pies

The breakfast dishes were cleared away the Wednesday before Thanksgiving. Brian Duffin cleared his throat with an air of gravity and announced, "The fifth annual Duffin Family Pie-making Festival is about to begin. I have observed that the chief purchasing officer has obtained all the necessary ingre-dients, and the members of the society are assembled. I officially acknowledge that we have a new member of the society, who has yet to declare her plan for her creation." He paused and looked significantly at

Rocky.

Rocky had been listening with interest. Mrs. Duffin had told her that Mr. Duffin loved to make pies the day before Thanksgiving, but when the attention was turned to her, she was flustered.

"Well, Rocky," Mr. Duffin's voice was very gentle as he spoke to her. "What kind of pie do you want to make for Thanksgiving?"

"I don't know." She stared at her worn sneakers.

Amber was beside her and commented, "You can make any kind you want, whatever is your favorite."

Rocky glanced up at Mr. Duffin. "I've only eaten punkin."

"Oh, my! An uninitiated member! She has only tried punkin, and she doesn't comprehend the possibilities! Will it be punkin, lemon or raspberry? Will she choose chocolate-mint, or coconut-cream? Could it be pecan or cheeseake with cherry or lemon meringue? What will her wild imagination concoct? Perhaps apple with cinnamon, or will she finally settle on the chief pie-maker's favorite, cranberry-apple with vanilla ice cream?

Rocky fidgeted her fingers and studied the bewildering pile of ingredients. "Can I watch and decide when I see what everyone else is doing? I don't really know how to make a pie," she added.

"Watch indeed. I understand you wish to witness the competition before your masterpiece is settled. Very well, we shall begin. First, Rocky, as our newest member, you shall produce the first pastry crust. I will supervise." Lillian loaded the necessary ingredients onto the table. She plugged in the electric mixer and laid out the measuring spoons and cups. Rocky cringed as Brian lifted her onto the chair at the head of the table, but he proceeded as though he didn't notice.

"First, you must measure three cups of this flour into the bowl." He showed her how to level the flour and dump it in. Her hands shook. "Now add one teaspoon of salt to the flour," he said as he pointed out the teaspoon. "Now add one cup and then one fourth cup of this nice, slimly, greasy, artery-clogging shortening!" He showed her how to wet the cups so the shortening would slip out. "Now turn the mixer onto the number 2, and when it looks like crumbs, turn it off. Rocky watched intently and then quickly turned it off at the correct instant. "Well done! You are obviously a great talent at cooking! Now crack this egg on the counter and add it to the dough." Rocky had to tap five times to get the egg cracked, but she pulled it apart without dropping any shell. "Well done again. You obviously have been practicing your cooking for many years to do it so well."

"I have never cooked like this before. In school we

made some stuff, but that was my very first egg to crack!"

"You are doing it really well, much better than when I started out." Kristin commented.

"Enough chit-chat," Mr. Duffin interjected. "You will disturb the concentration of my promising student! Rocky, add six tablespoons of this ice water." She measured carefully with the tablespoon indicated. "And last, one teaspoon of vinegar!" The little girl completed the task, and then looked up at her foster dad. He smiled at her, and she smiled faintly. "Now mix until it's all together like clay." Rocky watched carefully and again turned it off at just the right moment. "Perfect," Mr. Duffin cheered. "You're a natural!"

He encouraged her through the rolling and fitting, adding pressure on the rolling pin. Rocky showed that her hand had recovered from the weeks in the cast as she imitated Katy in crimping the crusts. The whole family admired the three neat crusts that stood ready for fillings.

"You're a born pie-maker! Now, while our assistants turn these into their masterpieces, we'll make some more crust." Brian was exultant, but Rocky breathed hard as though she had been exercising.

"Do I have to?" she asked Lillian. Lillian wiped her hands on her apron and came around the kitchen counter to the dining area where the others were working.

"You did a beautiful job on the pie crusts. Don't you want to make your own pie?"

Rocky bit her lower lip. "Can I go read my book in my room?"

Lillian and Brian exchanged glances, and Brian answered. "If you would like to go read that's okay, but we would sure love to have you stay out here with the rest of the family. I never saw anyone learn to make pie-crust so fast. They're pretty hard."

The little girl left the room. When Josh thought she was out of earshot he commented, "She's still so weird!"

Brian answered in a lowered voice. "I guess she does the best she can."

Rocky tiptoed up the stairs and shut the door to her room. She pressed Jamie's letter against her nose as she imagined that she could smell her mother on the paper. The longing rose in her body and ached in her stomach like an ulcer. She wondered where Jamie was going for Thanksgiving. *Has Grandma gotten well and forgotten to find me? Last year we went to the soup kitchen and ate lots of good food. Gramma laughed that there might not be room for all three of us in the truck after such a big dinner, but I rode home on Jamie's lap, and we fit just fine.*

She hugged her pillow as she remembered Jamie's

smell and how she liked to twirl Rocky's hair on her finger. After a few minutes, she thought about the pies they had at the soup kitchen. Jamie never cooked anything, and Rocky imagined how pleased she would be that her little girl could make pies. The child remembered herself serving Jamie some pie at Thanksgiving. She had wanted punkin with whipped cream. *Where, Where had she gone?*

Lillian went to Rocky's room after the rest of the family finished lunch. "Come have something to eat and see the pies you helped make."

Rocky shook her head, studying her shoes. Lillian noticed the rumpled envelope in her hand. "Is that the letter from your mom?"

Rocky nodded.

"May I see it?"

Rocky looked up as though startled and stuffed the letter under her summer shirt she had put on.

"Rocky, Miss Charlene told me about your letter, and she told me to ask you if I could see it. Since it is the only thing that your mama left before she disappeared, Miss Charlene hopes that there is some clue in it that will help us to find her. Does she say where she is going in the letter? Does she say anything about her plans or give any clues?" The child shook her head.

"It's possible that you don't understand something that is really a clue to finding her. If you let me read it, I'll stay right here in front of you." Rocky shook her head again. Lillian stepped toward her, feeling a little impatient after five months without any progress in finding her missing mother. Rocky drew back in fear. Lillian held out her hand, "Please, Rocky!" Rocky scooted backward across the bed.

Her impatience slipped into her voice, "Rocky, I don't want to have to wait until you're asleep. Miss Charlene needs to know what's in the letter so she can know what to plan for you. If your mom is coming back, you'll just stay here until she does. If she isn't coming back, your file will be changed, and Dad and I will file for adoption. We want to help you, and we want to do what's best!" Lillian knew that parental rights would be terminated soon without the letter, but she also knew it would be easier for the child if she was confident that there was no other way.

Lillian reached for the letter again, and Rocky leaped to the far side of the bed. Her eyes were blazing, and she yanked the letter out from under her shirt and tore into small pieces.

"Oh, Rocky, what have you done!"

"You can take it now!" She threw the handful of shredded paper toward Lillian.

"I'm sorry!" Lillian said. "I didn't think my reading it would hurt you." She went to her bedroom and brought back an envelope the same size as the original. "Keep the pieces in here so that you still have the letter, even if you can't read it." The little girl didn't reach for the envelope until Lillian shut the door behind her. She gathered the pieces into the envelope and then sank down weeping to the floor. Lillian came in again and reached down to comfort her, but Rocky recoiled. When Lillian had gone out again, Rocky buried her nose in the fresh envelope, but the new paper covered Jamie's smell. Rocky dumped the little pieces into the pillowcase.

At bedtime Lillian returned and placed a plate with a supper on it on the dresser. She watched Rocky pick at it. "Won't you come now to see the pies you helped make?" Lillian asked.

The little girl followed her to the buffet in the dining room that was covered with pies. Lillian pointed to a beautiful pecan, a lemon meringue and to a chocolate cream. "Aren't they nice?"

Just then Brian entered the dining room. "You helped make some of the best pies ever, Rocky!" He said. "I can hardly wait till tomorrow so that we can gobble them up after we gobble the gobbler! That pecan pie looks so good that you could sell it in a restaurant! Mmmm-mmmmm." The filling had caramelized around the edges of the golden brown crust.

Lillian broke the silence. "Rocky, we always like to take some pies to the soup kitchen in the morning of Thanksgiving. Would you like to help choose some? You can help deliver them too, if you want."

Rocky gasped in sudden joy. "You know about the soup kitchen?" she asked.

"Yes, of course! Every year after we bake pies in our Family Pie Festival, we choose our favorites and take them to the soup kitchen," Brian explained. "It's funny, but it makes the ones left at home taste even better. Would you like to go?"

"Oh, yes!" For an instant, the Duffins saw untainted delight in Rocky's face. "I'd like to go there more than anything in the whole world!"

"Have you been there before?" Lillian asked

"Yes, my mom and Grandma and I went on Thanksgiving last year. They had lots of good food. We rode in Grandma's truck."

"Did you have any lemon or pecan or pumpkin pie last year?" Brian asked.

"I had punkin. Remember, I *told* you!"

"Oh yes, only 'punkin'. You know what, Rocky, you probably ate a pie I made last Thanksgiving. What did your Mamma Jamie and Grandma have?"

"Mama Jamie had punkin, too, and Grandma had two kinds and one was lemon and I don't remember the other kind. They let me eat the white part on the lemon pie that tastes like marshmallow." Rocky was smiling.

"Then I think we should take that beautiful lemon pie that you helped make to the soup kitchen. We'll take some punkins, too, just in case there are other little girls there that want some. Sound good?"

Rocky blurted, "I might even *see* my mom there!"

"You might, Rocky. I would love to meet your mother. She must be a pretty nice girl to have raised a girl as good as you," Lillian said.

The real possibilities of the next day made Rocky philosophical. "She is a *very* nice girl, but she has some problems, too."

"We'd still like to meet her, wouldn't we, Brian?"

He nodded. "Maybe we'll get the chance in the morning."

Chapter 8

The Soup Kitchen

Rocky woke before sunup. She dressed in her best jeans and a blue sweater. She pulled her pink and orange flowered tank top over the sweater and hoped it would make it easier for Jamie to recognize her.

She tiptoed downstairs and was surprised to see Lillian wrestling a twenty-five-pound turkey into the roaster. Lillian smiled when she noticed her.

"You're up with us chickens! I've never had company

this early on Thanksgiving."

"I'm excited to take the pies. Will you have time to braid my hair this morning?"

"I'll make time. It is so fun to do your hair because it stays in so well. See, Dad made three more lemon and two more punkin pies last night so we could take them to the soup kitchen today. He stacked them in the pie carriers, see?"

Rocky climbed on a chair for a better view. She could tell that the lemon pie on top in the carrier was the one she had helped make. "What time are we going to the soup kitchen?"

"We'll leave at about 10:00. They want the pies delivered at 10:45. We'll eat breakfast, and then we'll have time to get the rolls going before we go." Lillian invited her to help stuff the turkey, and she enjoyed the strange task. When Lillian said, "It's time to sew up the turkey," the little girl thought she was joking. How strange she thought it was to watch her foster-mom close the skin over the stuffing with a needle and thread.

"I am practicing to be a doctor when I grow up," Lillian laughed. "But they'll only let me practice on turkeys."

Rocky smiled. Mrs. Duffin said funny things. She didn't usually laugh, but today she felt happy. It didn't seem long at all until Brian was loading the pies into the back of the van.

❧ ❧ ❧

They'd driven forty minutes when Rocky recognized the supermarket where Jamie used to shop. "My old school is right over there. See the flagpole? I can see where the buses park, too!" She had both her hands pressed against the window, despite the seat belts.

Brian turned the car quickly in the direction indicated. A chain-link fence topped with barbed wire surrounded the school. The front gate was padlocked, but they could see the low buildings arranged in a U around an asphalt playground. The sparse playground equipment was dilapidated. Yet Rocky's face shone with pleasure as she pointed out each familiar object. "That red door was where I had kindergarten, and the blue one next to it was first grade. I was the first one in my class to read!"

"I remember how well I loved my first school," Lillian commented. "My family was in the military, and so we moved often, but I always wished we could go back to that first school."

The other children were silent. Brian assured Rocky that it was a very nice school, and he could see why she liked it so much. Having circled the block, Brian turned back onto the boulevard, and they continued toward their destination. Rocky twisted in her seat to catch the last glimpse of it until it was hidden by the tiny houses that clustered near it.

Brian parked in the alley behind the soup kitchen. Rocky leaped from her seat and popped open the latch on the rear gate. She lifted her lemon pie off the top of the carrier and chose her footing carefully over the broken pavement. Brian held the door for her and she entered the dining hall looking about herself like a queen entering a drawing room. The lady wearing a white net on her hair was the same as last year.

"We have been hoping for some of the Duffin's special pies. It looks like you have really gone all out this year," the lady said.

The little girl smiled with pleasure. "I helped make some of them."

"Did you! They look delicious. There will be lots of hungry people today who are glad you're a good pie maker!"

"My other mom, Jamie brought me here before on Thanksgiving. I hope she comes today."

"I hope so too." The lady smiled.

Servers were carrying trays and bins of food to the serving tables and there were people waiting at the front door. The other Duffin children stood together in a tight cluster. Lillian spoke loudly to he husband. "They seem shorthanded. Shall we stay to help until our Turkey is ready?"

Rocky turned her hopeful face to her foster-parents.

"Sounds like fun, eh Rocky?" Brian grinned.

Rocky nodded happily.

The lady with the hairnet distributed matching hairnets to the family, and assigned Brian and Rocky to serve pie. Rocky cut the slice in the requested size, and Brian served it onto a little paper plate. Lillian stood on Brian's other side serving whipped cream and ice cream. Rocky was exact in finding the center of the pie so that the pieces would be symmetrical, but that didn't prevent her from keeping a close watch on the front door.

Three hours later, the crowd thinned. There were interruptions in the line now, and several tables were cleared and wiped without being reused. When there was nobody in line, the hairnet lady announced, "Closing time!" Rocky dropped her pie serving knife and rushed to the front of the soup kitchen, searching the empty street. She watched for several minutes, but finally retreated to where her family had gathered.

"I'm disappointed that I didn't get to meet your Mom Jamie today," Brian said. "I think I'll get to meet her some day, though."

Rocky dragged herself to her seat in the van. When they had passed the supermarket, she closed her eyes. She was asleep when they turned into their driveway.

Chapter 9

The Feast

Rocky woke on the living room couch when Amber touched her shoulder and told her it was time to eat. The smell of turkey hung thick in the air, and the pies they had saved at home were lined up on the sideboard. Rocky lingered over them for a moment.

"Hurry up!" Josh said. "I'm famished!" The little girl sat in her chair a little bewildered by the array of dishes on the table. The turkey was already cut up on a platter, and there were more dishes on a little side table that someone had set up while she was asleep.

"I hope it looks good to you, Rocky, because we're going to be eating this stuff until Christmas," Katy said.

"I'll say the blessing," Brian said and everyone bowed their heads. "Dear Father in Heaven . . ." he began, "We are grateful . . ." His voice caught in his throat, and he couldn't continue. Rocky heard Katy snicker, and she glanced around and saw that Brian had tears on his cheeks and a deep frown but the rest of the family were smiling. A full minute went by when he continued, ". . . for everything Thou hast given us. We are especially thankful this year." His voice went up in pitch and he paused again. ". . . for the new member of our family. Please help her, Lord to be happy and help each of us to do our best to show our gratitude . . ."

When the prayer was over, and Rocky saw that the family was still grinning, Josh explained. "Every year, Dad says the blessing at Thanksgiving and every year he gets all choked up and can barely say it."

"I'm sorry," Brian said.

"Why do we have Thanksgiving anyway," Rocky asked.

Lillian explained about the Pilgrims and Indians and about being grateful for blessings, adding that it was one of her very most favorite family traditions.

"I know of a tradition that other families have that I think we ought to try ourselves," Brian said as he served himself some potatoes and passed them to Katy. "In the Jew's culture, they watch for the prophet Elijah to come at their feast time. So they always set an extra plate for him. Rocky, what do you think about the idea of filling a Thanksgiving plate for your mom? We'll cover it really well and put it in the freezer. When the time comes that she can eat it, we'll bring it out, warm it up in the microwave and give it to her."

Josh shook his head, "Don't you think that's getting her hopes up too much?"

Lillian got a heavy paper plate from the cupboard and gave it to Rocky. "I think it's a good idea. We'll put it on paper so it can go in the microwave when the time comes, and it won't get broken if something bumps it," Lillian said. "Just put it beside your place and when things are passed to you, serve yourself and serve some for Mom Jamie. Just don't put the jello on there, since it will be ruined in the microwave." Rocky served both plates generously and wrapped the extra plate in plastic and then in foil. She placed it carefully on the top shelf of the freezer and returned to the table.

"That's good," she said softly to herself as she tasted the mashed potatoes.

Chapter 10

Illness

The Sunday after Thanksgiving, Amber woke with bloodshot eyes and a high fever. Rocky heard her throw up in the bathroom and then call, "Mama!" Rocky went in, filled a glass with water and gave it to her as she sat on the floor. "Rinse your mouth," she said. Amber obeyed.

"Please get Mama." Rocky nodded and went to Mr. and Mrs. Duffin's door. It was a little ajar, and she knocked lightly.

"Come in," Brian said. Rocky pushed the door open until she could see Lillian and Brian lying under the covers on their bed, but she didn't go further into the room.

"Amber needs you." She didn't address either of them specifically. "She's throwing up, and her forehead is hot."

"Oh, no," Lillian got out of bed, and Rocky watched as she pulled her robe over her long nightgown. She didn't look much like the ladies in the magazines that modeled "night wear."

Lillian picked up Amber and laid her on her bed. She took her temperature and said it was 103. "You're a sick little cookie," Lillian said. "Rocky, you better stay out of here so you don't catch sick."

"I won't," Rocky said. I never get sick anymore."

"Just to be safe, you stay out of here."

Rocky went to church with the rest of the family and when she got home, Amber was on Lillian's lap, her cheeks pale and her hair messy. Lillian glanced up with a brief smile and continued reading the storybook aloud. Rocky wished she would start over, since Cinderella was her favorite too, but Lillian went on.

Brian leaned over his wife's shoulder. "How's our

little squirt?" Lillian merely nodded to the thermometer on the chair beside her.

"103.7," he whistled. "Did you call the doctor?"

"There's a prescription waiting. Will you go pick it up?"

"Yep. I'll be right back."

"The children at church made fun of me because my hair wasn't combed," Rocky said. "Will you braid it for me?"

"Not now. I don't want to put Amber down. Go change out of your Sunday clothes." Rocky frowned but left without answering. A little later, she returned, wearing the grayish clothes she had worn the day she went to the hospital.

"I told you that you could keep those if you wouldn't wear them anymore. They're too small, and it's not the right season for them," Lillian said.

"I like them." Rocky went into her own room and shut the door with as much emphasis as she could. She waited for half an hour, expecting Lillian to come reason with her, but when she didn't come, Rocky went downstairs again and found Katy. "Remember you told me you'd teach me to ride Amber's old bike? Can we do it now?"

"No, Rocky. It has flat tires and Amber needs to give

you permission, and she's sick."

"I can pump them up. Kristen showed me how."

"I don't want to do it right now. I'm worried about Amber."

"You're selfish," Rocky said.

"No, *honey*, I'm not selfish. I'm worried." Rocky knew when she said 'honey' she meant the opposite.

Rocky found Josh writing in his little leather-bound book. "Will you help me ride the bike? Katy won't."

"Nope. I don't think you should ride Amber's bike when she's so sick. It's sleeting a little outside, too, so nobody wants to go out. Why are you dressed like that, anyway?"

"I like it."

"I thought Mom told you to change."

"I didn't want to."

Rocky went to her room and read the book about the lost mouse. When she finished, she went outside, rolled Amber's bike to the front sidewalk and sat on it. She couldn't get it to move, so she rolled it to the top of the driveway where there was enough slope to roll it.

She lifted her feet and the floppy tires began to turn.

The front tire wobbled so much that she put her feet down to keep from falling, but the bike rolled faster. Just then, Brian pulled into the driveway and was forced to yank the car sideways and brake with a screech to avoid hitting her.

"What are you doing!" He was angry. Rocky stared at him silently. "I asked you a question! What are doing on Amber's bike, with flat tires, dressed like it's June!" He had never raised his voice to her before.

"Nobody would help me. They're too selfish."

Katy had come from the house when she heard the commotion. "Maybe it's time you realized that you're not the only one in the world. What if Amber dies? How would you feel?"

"You put that bike away right now and get upstairs to your room," Brian commanded.

Rocky wheeled the bike to the back yard and threw it down. She banged the back door and banged her bedroom door. Lillian called her from Amber's room. Amber seemed to be asleep on her lap. Josh was there, looking angrily at her, and Brian didn't look at her at all as he prepared a dose of medicine.

"I want you to get some fresh bedding from the linen closet and make Amber's bed. Josh will show you where to find it. Put the dirty sheets in the hamper. Then go change your clothes like I told you."

Josh gave her two sheets and a pillow case, and she went into Amber's room. It smelled bad. Amber had wet the bed and gotten some vomit on it too. Rocky stood motionless beside it for awhile. Finally she said, "Amber wet the bed."

"I know. Children often do when they're sick."

"I quit wetting the bed when I was two."

"Don't say too much before you have the flu. Get the bed taken care of so Amber will have a clean place to lie."

"She's being a big baby," she said as she peeled the bed. There was a plastic mattress protector under the sheet. She grumbled as she stretched the fresh bottom sheet. "Why do I have to take care of her pee-bed when I don't wet my bed? Baby, baby, baby."

"No, she's not! Won't you help her without being mean to her?"

"I'm not being mean to her. Everyone is being mean to me." She spread the upper sheet and found fresh blankets folded under the bed. She lowered her voice. "She keeps blankets here because she pees in the bed all the time, 'cuz she's a baby, baby, baby." She pulled up the bedspread and put Molly Dolly upside down on the pillow.

"I don't think so, Sister," Brian said. If you can't be nice, go to your room and shut the door without slamming it."

Rocky obeyed, but later refused to eat the turkey sandwiches Kristen brought her in her room. Kirsten carried them down again. She heard Lillian put Amber in her bed and later Rocky listened while the family had pie. Nobody called her or came up to talk to her. It was almost bedtime when she went downstairs and cut herself a piece of pie.

"You can have pie when you have changed out of those clothes," Lillian said.

Rocky continued serving herself without answering Lillian. When she turned toward her room with her plate in hand, Brian rose from his seat in the living room and blocked her passage upstairs.

"Go put down the pie until you've changed out of those clothes like your mother said." She went to the table but continued to hold her plate for a minute, looking angrily from Lillian to Brian. She banged it on the table, splattering it onto Josh and Kristen, and began to cry.

Brian strode to her, scooped her up in one arm and carried her, kicking and struggling to her room. "You picked a heck of a day to fall apart, Rocky. It's time you thought of someone else besides yourself for once." He tried to set her down standing, but she buckled her knees and collapsed in a melodramatic heap. He shut the door behind himself as she wailed at the top of her voice. He opened the door again. "You keep your voice down, so you don't disturb Amber." She scowled, but lowered her voice.

When Lillian didn't come after 15 minutes, Rocky opened her door and wailed, "I don't want to starve! Please don't starve me!" She hadn't known that Lillian was in her own bedroom, and she came out directly. "You change your clothes and go eat your supper, or just get to bed now."

Rocky shut her door softly, slipped into her nightgown and crawled into bed without saying her prayers or brushing her teeth. She lay in the bed, listening and angry.

It was very late when she heard Brian instructing Kristen in a hushed frightened voice. "Keep an eye on Rocky, so she doesn't do anything, and we'll call you as soon as we know anything. Brian and Lillian moved into Amber's room, and she heard them go downstairs. After the door to the garage closed, she looked out her window where she had a view of the street. As the family car went under the streetlight, she could see Lillian and Brian, but nobody else. She looked in Amber's room but the bed was empty. She went downstairs to where Kristen watched the empty street from the living room window.

"Where are they going?" She was frightened.

"They're taking Amber to the hospital. Her fever was too high and the medicine wasn't helping." Kristen had tears on her cheeks.

"Is she going to die?"

Kristen looked back into the cold night. "I don't know." She was crying.

Rocky crossed the room and stood beside her, listening to her quiet weeping. She put her arm around her waist and buried her face in Kirsten's flannel nightgown. "I'm sorry I was a brat, today," she said softly.

"I hope you'll do better tomorrow," Kirsten said. She patted Rocky's back gently, and the little girl shed genuine, worried tears.

Chapter 11

Amber

Rocky was asleep on Kristen's lap when the phone rang on Monday morning. Katy and Josh were dressed and eating breakfast in the kitchen. Katy answered. Dad's voice was strained. Amber had been admitted, and the doctors and nurses were giving her fluids intravenously. They said she had influenza and that Mom would stay with her for the day and Dad would stay with her at night.

"Is she going to be all right?" Josh asked.

Katy held up her hand so she could hear. She listened and nodded and hung up.

"Dad says that they think she'll be okay, but that she'll have a hard couple days still. But he said a little girl died of the flu last night, just two doors down the hall." Her face crumpled and she covered it with her hand.

"She'll be all right," Kristen said as she put her arms around Katy, Rocky and Josh at once. We need to pray for her and have faith."

Rocky was vividly aware of every point of contact on her body as she stood in the collective embrace. She could smell Josh's breath and a trace of the perfume Katy had worn to church the day before. She felt herself getting weak and a little wobbly, like a Popsicle in the embrace of sparklers. She couldn't help disliking the closeness any-more than they could help the warmth they produced.

Just when Rocky felt she must squirm free, Kristen released them, directing them to kneel. She took Rocky's hand in hers and the little girl immediately offered her other hand to Katy. Josh held both his sister's hands.

Kristen directed the others to kneel with her, and she said the prayer. Rocky felt better after that and went up to dress herself without being told. She put on her best school clothes and as she started to drop her nightgown into the hamper, she noticed the old grayish clothes that she had worn the day before. She picked them up from the floor and dropped them in the trash can.

As she held Kristen's hand on the way to school, she asked, "Do you think my mom Jamie prayed for me when I was in the hospital?"

"I think," Kristen answered slowly, "that many things would be different for you if your mother had known how to pray."

Rocky thought about it the rest of the way to school, and just before Kristen released her hand, she squeezed her eyes shut and whispered quickly, "God, help my mom and Amber!" Whether Kristen had heard or not, she couldn't tell, but she didn't mind the quick kiss on her cheek that Kristen left her with.

❧ ❧ ❧

Rocky barely saw Lillian and Brian for the next several days. When Kristen heard that Amber could come home on Friday, she and Katy bought crepe paper streamers and helium balloons and let Rocky help them decorate the house and paint a *Welcome Home Amber* banner. Josh said it was "girl style," but when it was ready, he said it looked good. All four of them stood at the front window waiting, and they cheered when they saw them turn the corner of their street. As Dad carried Amber in from the garage, very pale and weak, but smiling, an unexpected surge of gladness filled her chest and made tears form in her eyes. Suddenly, she thought of what had happened the night she went to the hospital many months before when she was filled with light and music. Amber seemed like one of those who were dressed in white who had welcomed her in the place where there wasn't any pain. She grabbed Amber's foot as Brian carried her past and kissed it. Lillian laughed, and Rocky laughed, too, but she wasn't embarrassed. She wondered why she hadn't thought about the beautiful place much lately.

Chapter 12

Gifts

Rocky worked hard at school. And after her week of worry about Amber, she smiled more. Sometimes she gave her teacher, Mrs. Trout, small scraps of memories from her earlier school that she had not told the Duffins, and little by little a clearer image of what she had endured emerged. Academically, she was advanced enough to move to an older grade, but Mrs. Trout and the Duffins agreed that she shouldn't be rushed.

Rocky was pleasant with her classmates but didn't draw close to any particular child. She never asked another child to be her partner but waited for her teacher to assign her.

The current of excitement for the holidays made the second graders squirmy. It was as though someone had wired a low electric charge through all the chairs that made it hard to stay in a seat for longer than a few seconds, and the talking during "quiet" times was often better described a "din" than a "hum". Rocky knew from her classmates that they were used to much more elaborate celebrations than anyone even imagined in her earlier school, and the Duffins had mentioned traditions that were foreign to her, too.

Amber had asked her what she wanted for Christmas from her. She didn't know, but she soon understood that the family would exchange gifts. She needed something for each of the Duffins, and she wondered how she would get presents for them when they gave her everything she had.

Hope sparked when Mrs. Trout announced that the next day would be a day when the whole class would make gifts for their families. After school, she asked the teacher what she meant, and Mrs. Trout explained that the children could make things to give as gifts. They would be allowed to make as many things as they had time for.

"Oh, I've been so worried. This is a big relief!" She said it so earnestly that her teacher laughed. Though Rocky didn't understand why, she smiled at her too.

When she arrived at class the next day, she found it arranged in stations for a variety of projects. She was attracted first to the sock-puppet table. It didn't look too hard, and she was doubly pleased to find a pink sock, since pink was Amber's favorite color. For a moment, she stopped to imagine what Amber would say when she opened it, and then sat down to assemble the best puppet ever made. She followed the instructions minutely, and the end result had braided yarn hair, a tiny straw hat and googly eyes. Rocky riveted her eyes on her sneakers when Mrs. Trout admired it and showed it to the rest of the class as a good example.

Rocky moved around the room in search of a second project. Some kids were painting coffee mugs. The Duffins mostly used plastic cups, and she didn't think they would like one of those. There were felt "dust bunnies" for dusting, but Rocky knew that Amber always did the dusting and it didn't seem like much of a gift. When Rocky noticed a table where kids were making picture frames, her interest was sparked. She recognized them as similar to the row of frames on the fireplace mantel. The kids were gluing small sea shells onto cardboard frames until they were entirely covered. They put a picture of themselves in the frame and put a back on it with a brace so that it would stand. Rocky studied the sample.

"If you want to make a frame, I'll take your picture with my digital camera, and then you can glue it in," Mrs. Trout suggested.

"Do you think that the Duffins would want a picture of me?" she asked.

"Of course they would! They'd love it. I know that their older kids have been in my class, and they have given one just like this to them."

"I know. They have them on the top of the fireplace. But I don't know if they would want one of *me."*

"Why don't you take a chance and find out." Mrs. Trout lifted the little chin. "Don't you know that the Duffins love you?"

Rocky pulled her chin free and pretended to examine a stray seashell. She shook her head.

Mrs. Trout patted the child on the shoulder. "Go ahead and make the frame. I know that they will love to look at it on their mantel with all of their other children."

Was it true? Rocky wondered. *Do they think of me the way they thought of Amber?* It didn't seem possible. She didn't feel the same way about them as she did about Mom Jamie. She felt Mrs. Trout watching her, so she began to glue with unsteady fingers. She made sure that no cardboard was visible anywhere and that the glue didn't drip.

When Mrs. Trout poised the camera, Rocky smiled her prefab paper-doll smile. "I don't flash until I see a real smile on your pretty face." The comment drew a shy, closed-lip smile, and Mrs. Trout snapped the picture. As she watched the image emerge from the printer, it looked similar to one that Gramma had on her shelf that was of Jamie when she was little.

"Now *that's* a cute picture!" the teacher said.

"I think so, too."

She glued in the photograph and then put on the back. Rocky guarded the creation as the glue dried so that nothing would slip. When the seashells were set, Rocky moved it to the drying table to wait for wrapping the next day. When the time came, she was faced with a new dilemma she had not anticipated. She didn't know what she ought to put on the card for her foster parents. Finally, she asked Mrs. Trout about it.

"They're not my real parents, but their other kids call them 'Mom' and 'Dad'," she explained.

"Why not just put 'Mom Lillian and Dad Brian'. Remember that they know that they didn't have you as a baby. But don't worry too much and just write whatever you feel good about."

Lillian met her at the front door that afternoon. "I think that today is the day you were going to bring home presents from school. If it's what I hope it is, I can hardly wait to put it in the special place we put such things." She glanced at the mantel, and Rocky's face brightened.

"Do you want to see it? It's all wrapped up."

"Sure! I promise I won't peek inside, even if I'm tempted." Lillian took the little package wrapped with heavy green paper and tied with red yarn. She read the card aloud. "*To Mom Lillian and Dad Brian from Rocky.* Oh it's perfect! I can hardly wait. It feels like it might just be what we have been wanting!"

Rocky took back the little present with a smile and hurried to secure her treasures in her bedroom. She slipped the cache into her pillowcase.

Chapter 13

The Christmas Program

The evening of the annual Christmas play was always somewhat hectic, but this year was chaotic. Mrs. Duffin was struggling to arrange Kristin's hair according to the director's instructions as Kristin was playing Mrs. Cratchett in the Community production of *A Christmas Carol*. Josh was going to run the spotlight and was urging everyone to hurry. Brian Duffin helped Amber get ready. Though Rocky's dress was laid on the bed with her socks and shoes, she sat beside it without moving.

"Mom, Rocky isn't getting ready!" Josh moaned. Just then the hairdo Lillian was struggling with collapsed, and Mrs. Duffin growled in frustration.

"Rocky, get those clothes on your bed onto your body now!" Mrs. Duffin commanded from the bedroom. "We absolutely cannot be late!" Still, Rocky stared at the blue and white dress.

"Rocky, hurry!" Mrs. Duffin called again.

Rocky shuffled to the bathroom door. "I don't want to wear that dress."

"Then find something else that is nice for the play, but be quick!"

Rocky went to the closet and pulled out one of her summer outfits. It was one of the shorts sets she had insisted Lillian buy her when they went school shopping. She donned her frilly socks and black patent leather shoes. Then she reverently drew her pink purse from her bottom drawer. It had her ten-dollar bill zipped into the pocket, and she pirouetted in front of the mirror. She knew she was supposed to wear a skirt, so she slipped a very short jumper over her head. The shorts hung well below the hem. "Somebody needs to button my dress," she said.

Brian finished with Amber and hurried into Rocky's room. "Did I hear you say you need buttoning? Dad to the rescue!" As he buttoned her jumper, she studied her socks.

"Did Mom say it was okay for you to wear your summer clothes tonight?" Dad asked.

"I didn't ask her because she's busy. I don't want to wear that other dress. It doesn't go with my purse. It's a set.

"Oh, yes, I see the dilemma. Well, you look pretty, and it is too late to change. Hold still so I can fix your hair." He grabbed her brush from the little vanity and fastened it back with a pink lace barrette. "Perfect." The little girl was self-conscious as Mr. Duffin touched her head, but it only took a few seconds.

"Now grab your coat and jump in the car."

The rest of the family rushed into the car with her, and they arrived at the school auditorium exactly on time.

The participants found their designated meeting places, and the remaining family chose seats on the aisle near the front. When Mrs. Duffin noticed what was under Rocky's coat, she looked wearily to Brian. "A little over-dressed, don't you think?"

"Not a bit. She needed to bring her Christmas money in her purse, and since she only has one purse, she had to wear the pink shorts to go with it."

"And you added the frilly barrette to complete the ensemble. I understand perfectly!"

"Well, the easiest way to disarm an opponent is to sneak up behind and hit them in their weak spot. Why do you think I buy you chocolate?" Lillian rolled her eyes, but smiled as Rocky arranged the folds of her skirt so that her shorts would show. Amber sat beside Rocky looking jealous of her outfit, but acting superior. "She looks silly," she muttered. "Mom never lets me wear my Sunday dresses to school when I want to." If Rocky had known the term "sour grapes" she would have suggested it to Amber, but she ignored her and enjoyed the sense of superior fashion the more.

At last the play began. The Duffins were soon engrossed in the familiar plot and Rocky was fascinated by it too, but she had forgotten to use the restroom before she came and she, squirmed in her seat. She watched until she knew she would be sorry if she waited one minute more and finally tiptoed out of the auditorium. A breezeway connected the auditorium to the school building and arrows directed the audience to the nearest restroom in the school, since the actors were using the ones near the auditorium for costuming.

The air was biting cold outside, and she shivered. The school door was so heavy that Rocky had to brace herself to push it open, and the restroom was at the far end of the dimly-lit hall. Rocky rushed toward it. The door latch stuck and the delay was disastrous. Her panties, shorts and socks were wet, and she let out a desperate sob. It would soon begin to smell bad, and besides, she didn't want to miss any more of her first play! The door latch released, and she rushed into the bathroom. She removed her under things and socks and rinsed them with soap in the sink. She held the clothing under the hand dryers, but it took fifteen minutes for the clothing to dry enough to put back on. *It was still a little damp, but at least it would not stink,* she thought.

She grabbed her purse and struggled past the heavy door. She began to run down the hall, but then stopped halfway. A cluster of teenage boys had formed between her and the door to the breezeway. She started forward, but her shoes clattered on the hard, linoleum floor though she tried to walk quietly. Their earrings shone in the flicker of their cigarette lighters. They were using words that she remembered from when she lived at the trailer. They were words the man with the yellow car used often, and her first grade teacher told her that she must never ever say them.

Their cigarettes smelled sickly sweet, and she recognized their twisted ends as they passed them to each other. A boy wearing a spiked dog-collar noticed her.

"Look, it's Cinderella." The boys glanced around.

"What do you have in your little purse there, baby?"

The boy with the dog-collar questioned her. Rocky clutched the purse and stared at the big boy.

Slowly he moved toward her, and she backed away. He quickened his step. "Let me see it, baby."

Rocky turned and ran back toward the girl's bathroom with a little scream. To her horror, Dog-collar Boy followed her into the bathroom and yanked the purse from her hands. He snapped it open and seized the new bill. The ten dollars disappeared into his shirt pocket as he surveyed her with narrowed eyes. Rocky was dizzy with fear. She shrank as small as she could and tried to scream, but her voice was strangled in her constricted throat. The bathroom light was harsh but she saw a gray haze. She tried to scream again but only whimpered. She was vaguely aware of running footsteps in the hall outside the bathroom, but she startled violently when the bathroom door slammed open and the boy jumped back.

"ROCKY!" a man's voice roared. Brian rushed further into the room and Dog-Collar dropped the pink purse to the floor with a clatter. The teen's eyes traveled involuntarily to the cowering little girl, and Brian followed his gaze. He grabbed the little girl into his arms and pressed her to his shoulder. "Are you hurt, Rocky? Did he hurt you? Are you okay, honey?" His voice trembled with concern. Rocky clung to Brian's neck, staring at the dark-clothed teenager behind him.

"He took my purse and my money," Rocky whispered. "He was going to hurt me."

Brian whirled on the pimply-faced kid. "Give it back now!" he commanded.

A surly expression flashed in the boy's face. "I ain't got nothin' of hers."

Brian pointed to the purse at his feet. "Give it to me now!" He demanded obedience. The sullen teen picked up the purse and handed it roughly to Brian. He tried to brush past him, but Brian blocked his way to the door. When he found the purse empty, he said, "She had ten bucks in here, and now it's gone. Give it to her now, or I'll take it from you.

"I ain't got nothin'."

"Maybe it was twenty bucks. Let me think?"

"I said I ain't got it!"

"Maybe it was thirty."

Brian noticed the bill showing over the edge the kid's shirt pocket and snatched it before Dog-Collar could react. "We'll take this then, to pay the little girl for your being such a jerk."

"That *is* my money, Dad." Rocky murmured.

"I know it is, honey."

Brian turned back to the boy. "You go home and don't come back tonight. If I see you here again, I'll file charges for assault." He pointed ahead as he pressed Rocky to his shoulder like she was a baby, and he followed the boy toward the door. The knot of boys parted silently as they passed.

※ ※ ※

Lillian was amazed to see Brian carry Rocky into the auditorium pressed to his shoulder. She could not question him without disturbing the audience, so she was left to wonder throughout the evening at how the fearful little child had been brought to nestle on his lap. Amber climbed on his opposite knee and assumed a similar position, and Brian did not shift his load or lighten his lap for the remaining hour. Meanwhile, Rocky was riveted on a little crippled boy, a miserly old man and a feeling of safety and warmth.

※ ※ ※

Rocky explained to the family what happened when they were gathered at home. She omitted why she needed to rinse her clothes, but all but Amber understood. When Lillian hinted, Rocky looked embarrassed, but Amber blurted, "I just take off my stuff when that happens." The family laughed.

"I can only imagine how scared you must have been," Katy commented. "I think we should call the police and tell them what happened."

"I wish I had been there, too. I would bust that guy in the nose." Josh still enjoyed his seventh-grade bravado.

"There is no need to get violent, Josh," Dad chided. "I did just fine by myself. I have to admit though, if that kid had pushed just one inch farther, he would have a big bald spot on his technicolor head."

As Lillian tucked Rocky into bed, she ventured a kiss on the child's flushed cheek.

"Do you know what, Mamma Lillian? My Mamma Jamie told me that men and big boys hurt girls if they can. She told me not to ever let a man come near me when I was alone and to always lock the door if she was not there. But Mamma Jamie didn't know any *good* men like Dad. I don't think *he* would *ever* hurt me . . ." Her voice trailed off.

Lillian brushed the hair off of Rocky's forehead. "Dad would never hurt you, Rocky. There are *many* good men and boys in the world. It's Dad's and my job to keep you safe until you are old enough to tell who is good and safe and who is not. We want to protect you, and you must not wander away from us. We were very scared when we saw that you had disappeared, and Amber knew that you had been gone for quite a while." Rocky pulled the covers up over her head.

"Goodnight, honey. I'm glad you're safe."

"Goodnight, Mama Lillian."

Chapter 14

Heaven

Rocky lay awake for a long time with conflicting emotions churning in her breast. The memory of her terror in the dimly lit hallway was over-shadowed by the relief and comfort of Brian's strong arms sweeping her up to safety. She had felt more safe and protected than ever before as she sat on his lap. His skin smelled clean like the doctor at the hospital, and, to her sensitive nose, it made a difference between him and other men she had been near. She considered that The Fat Man had never hurt her, but he never smelled good. But the memory of Jamie's warnings were still powerful. "Men will hurt you if you let them near you. They hurt me so bad in a private way that I can't even tell you. Lock the door and never let a man in, no matter what!" But Jamie would often leave her at night with the door unlocked.

Rocky was sure that Lillian was right, and Brian was a different kind of man than Jamie knew. *He smells good, he doesn't drink booze. He's clean and nice to his family and he's nice to me. But then again, what if he's pretending to be nice so that he could hurt me?* She puzzled with the thought that Amber had lived with both Josh and Brian her whole life, and she sat on their laps all the time. If they hurt Amber in that secret, private way, Amber would be afraid of them. But she wasn't. She played with her dad, and they *both* laughed all the time. She also remembered Amber bringing story books to Josh. He read to her whenever she asked. On Sundays, after Church and dinner, they always read out of a special book, and Amber liked to sit on a vacant lap, it didn't seem to matter whose. Rocky suddenly felt terribly empty. She was not a part of the family. She couldn't climb up on Lillian's or Brian's or the older children's lap like Amber did. She was suddenly alone again in a house full of people.

But the taste of genuine affection she had understood, even briefly that evening, left her hungry for more, but without enough experience to know how to obtain it. She wondered if it was even safe to obtain it at all?

Suddenly her bedroom door opened. Rocky's eyes widened as somebody tiptoed into her room. She didn't turn, but held her breath until Amber's tousled head moved around the corner of her bed into view. Rocky relaxed. Amber had a pillow under her arm and climbed into the warm bed beside Rocky. She pushed her pillow against Rocky's, and then the older girl felt a soft peck of a kiss on her cheek. "I don't want you to be scared anymore." Amber settled down beside her in the dark and fell asleep.

Rocky felt strange with Amber in bed with her, but the younger girl's even breathing soon lulled her to sleep.

She was in the place where there was beautiful singing and music flowing like water. Everyone was dressed in white, and she knew where she was. But this time, Rocky stood outside an archway looking in. She heard the music and singing, and it seemed to go to the center of her body. She wanted to drink it and be filled up. She remembered that they were singing about someone wonderful who was the source of the music like a spring issues a stream. It was so delicious that she couldn't hear it enough. But she could not go farther, and she could not be satisfied. She watched and yearned and listened like a thirsty traveler who can see the clear, clean water but cannot reach it.

She noticed a lady walking toward her. At first she thought it was the same white lady that had brought her back to her trailer that night, but when she looked into the lady's face she recognized her Grandma.

"Rocky, I must say goodbye." The child didn't understand what she meant. "I've left my body on the Earth. I was sick and that's why I couldn't come help you when you needed me. Now I have something important to tell you."

"What is it?" Rocky whispered, fearing the answer.

"You are safe with the Duffins. God prepared them and sent them to you. They already love you and will help you have a happy life as Roxanne Leila Duffin."

"Jamie said that men will hurt me, and I should never let them near me."

"Bad men hurt Jamie, and she had seen me hurt, too. She didn't know that there were good people like the Duffins who only want to love you and take good care of you. I came back to tell you this."

"Are you going to live here forever now?"

"Until The Life Giver returns to the Earth. When He returns, everyone will live again. I must leave you now, little Roxanne Leila. I love you."

"Does the Life Giver make the music?" She waved

her hand, indicating the whole of the scene she could see through the arch.

"Yes, Roxanne, He makes the music and the light and the love. The Duffins will teach you of Him. I must go now."

The music died away and Rocky's view darkened. She opened her eyes and the early morning sun was streaming in the window saluting the first day of Christmas vacation.

Chapter 15

The Call

The rising sun did not fade the profound reverence Rocky felt. Amber awoke a few minutes later and began listing all the fun things they had planned for Christmas, but the excited chattering did not penetrate her thoughts. Grandma had not forgotten her. Grandma said she loved her and that she wanted her to love the Duffins. Amber sat close, and Rocky smiled at her as her warmth penetrated her awareness. She liked the friendly feeling as Amber chattered, but wished she could be alone to think and remember, too. There was a new feeling inside, and she wanted to tell Lillian about it. She knew that the white world she had twice seen was not a mere dream, and she wanted to tell the message she had received. *How do you tell someone that you are new inside?* The gnawing pain that had been her companion for six months was noticeably duller. There was another new feeling of hope that Rocky searched unsuccessfully for a way to explain.

Rocky heard Lillian fixing breakfast in the kitchen. Amber's monolog about gingerbread houses continued, but the older girl excused herself and hurried into the bathroom. Amber was dressing in her own room when she returned. She heard Lillian answer the phone as she also began to dress.

❧ ❧ ❧

Lillian recognized Charlene Hollister's voice before she identified herself. After the necessary polite inquires, Charlene said, "Mrs. Duffin, I have something I need to inform you about. Rocky's grandmother died yesterday. Since Jamie Davis has never made any effort to contact Rocky for over six months and her only known relative is gone, she can now be officially moved into the Foster-adopt program."

Miss Charlene went on to explain that once the Duffins signed the necessary paperwork, the State would then file a motion to terminate parental rights. "Jamie actually has up to a full year to get her act together, but as nobody knows where she is, or even if she is alive, it looks like we could finalize the adoption after she has been with you twelve months.

ക ക ക

Rocky did not intend to eavesdrop, but she knew instinctively that the call had to do with her. She recognized the note of pleasure in Lillian's voice. "Absolutely yes! We'll come down first thing tomorrow if you can get the papers ready to sign. Thank you, so much!"

Rocky listened at the door to her foster parents' bedroom when she heard Lillian calling Brian at work. Lillian noticed her and smiled as she scooted her out and shut the door. She lowered her voice so that Rocky could not hear her at all.

In a moment she hurried in to Rocky's bedroom. She asked Amber to go out and close the door, and Amber obeyed. There was muted excitement in Lillian's face, but her little foster daughter was calm.

"I have some important news, Rocky." She sat down on the bed beside Rocky. "The phone call that just came was from Miss Charlene, the social worker. She said that your . . ."

"My Gramma died," Rocky interrupted. Lillian looked

surprised.

"Did you hear me talking?"

"No, I heard you on the phone, but I already knew." She lifted her face to look into Lillian's eyes. "My Gramma visited me last night. She is in a beautiful place, and she wears a white dress like everybody else there." Rocky wanted to release the flood of explanation and questions that filled her mind, but she stopped short, watching for some encouragement.

"Can you tell me what she said?" Lillian's voice was restrained.

"She said that you love me." Rocky's voice was barely above a whisper. "She said that you were my new family, and that I would be happy with you. She called me Roxanne Leila Duffin."

"Oh, Rocky! We *do* love you! I think your Grandma was sent from God to tell you!"

"Yes! She *told* me that God had given you to me."

"Sweetie, Dad and I already knew that God had sent you to us. You have been so good for us and especially for Amber. You have no idea how grateful we are for you. We want you to be part of our family *forever*, but we'll wait for Dad to get home to talk to you about that more. Was there anything else that you remember that you can share with me?"

"Yes! There was a lot more, but it's hard to explain. There's music everywhere and very white light, and you feel safe there. Everything comes from Him!"

"Who is He, Rocky?" Lillian's voice was full of wonder.

"Grandma called Him the Life Giver." Tears were in Rocky's eyes, "I wanted to see *Him*, but I didn't know how to find Him!"

Lillian smiled through her own tears. "I know who He is, and I know how to find Him. We will teach you about Him, and all that He has given us. It is so special and important to us that I know that Dad would be very sorry to miss telling you about Him. But for now," she stroked the flaxen hair as she tried to speak, "His name is Jesus."

Chapter 16

Jamie

Rocky's Grandma had lived in the same apartment building for many years and her friends met the news of her death with sorrow. They had known her to be a quiet, generous, uncom-plaining woman. They organized a grave-side service with a minister from a nearby chapel. They also arranged for a tender obituary in the newspaper. It was this obituary that The Fat Man happened to read, and he recognized the name. "Hmm," was the extent of the comment it drew from him.

The next day he was lounging in the tiny office with his booted feet on the counter when Jamie walked in. Her hair hung in greasy strings, and her flannel shirt was pitifully thin for the chilly weather. There were dark circles under her eyes, and her skin was more sallow than ever.

"I need some help, Jerry," She stated.

The Fat Man surveyed her coolly. "Ya look bad, babe. What da ya want?"

"First, I need to clean up. I want to find my baby."

"Yer mom died."

Jamie shrugged. "I thought she would."

"Rocky came here with a social worker after she got out of the hospital. I gave her yer letter."

"Thanks. I knew Rocky didn't die. I called the hospital, and she answered the phone in her room. I just hung up."

"Mmmm. She was pretty broken up, not seeing you."

"I want to see her now."

"You can see her at yer mom's funeral tomorrow. The paper says it's at Evergreen at two o'clock."

Jamie thought for a moment. "Do ya think that the

cops will be there to arrest me for what I done to Rocky, ya know, using the funeral as a trap?"

"I don't think anybody would spend that much trouble on ya, babe. I'll take you on the Harley if you wanna go."

"Can I clean up here?"

"Go ahead. My brother left shampoo and soap in there last week. Help yourself."

Chapter 17

Graveside

Lillian took Rocky to the department store early the next morning. She purchased a navy-blue sailor dress with white tights and black shoes. She also bought her a dressy coat and a matching hat. She helped her dress in the dressing room and then paid for the clothing with the tags. She allowed Rocky to carry the summer clothes she had worn into the store in her hands. Rocky folded them together so that the pink and orange pattern showed on the outside. Lillian also wore a dark blue dress with a white collar and a long, wool coat.

The wind blew in icy gusts as the pair crossed the frozen grass to the open grave. There was a little knot of people already there, and many of them stared at the well-dressed pair. At last, one neighbor recognized Rocky and murmured, "Sorry about yer grandma."

Rocky stared at the coffin. "Is Gramma's body in there?"

"Yes, Rocky, I think it is," Lillian said.

❧ ❧ ❧

Jamie wrapped herself in an old wool blanket The Fat Man had given her. Her hands were blue with the cold. She envied the face-covering helmet Jerry wore, for her head was bare.

"Don't forget to stop at the corner. I want to make sure it's safe before I go over. The Harley's so noisy that it'll warn everyone if we go all the way to the grave." The Fat Man nodded, and the motorcycle roared to life. Jamie clung to the broad back, her head bent against the wind.

The Fat Man stopped at the far corner of the cemetery before any of the mourners heard the roar. Jamie swung her leg over and asked, "You *are* going to wait for me, aren't you?" The black helmet nodded.

Rocky's back was to the wind and also away from the far corner where The Fat Man waited. The wind whipped and howled around the bare ash trees. It was hard to hear the Twenty-third Psalm that the minister was reading, but the assembled neighbors stared at the ground respectfully.

Jamie walked steadily toward the cluster of mourners. She could tell that the service had started, but she didn't hurry. She was studying the group, knowing that Rocky may not even know about her grandma's death. Then she caught sight of the child wrapped in a warm winter coat with a hat. She couldn't see her face, but even from a distance she noticed the bright orange and red bundle that was tucked under the little arm. The child held some white flowers in her other gloved hand. Jamie slipped behind the trunk of an old tree, watching her daughter. Lillian had a protective hand on her shoulder, and Jamie could see a little bit of the small woman's face. She could see her large eyes and understood the body language as the woman frequently glanced at Rocky's face. Tears welled up in Jamie's eyes. "I've lost my baby forever. She is that woman's girl now." Jamie's whisper drowned in the wind, but she added, "I could at least say goodbye to her the way I shoulda done before. I could hug her just one more time." She studied the little figure with longing. The wind caught Rocky's curled hair and blew it back lightly over her coat. How long it was! It seemed like such a short time since she had seen the little girl, though it seemed like forever that she had been hiding from the police.

When the sermon ended, Jamie took a step from

behind the tree. The little girl laid the white flowers on the coffin and then slipped her hand into Lillian's. The two turned away from the grave and walked away from where Jamie was standing. Jamie took another step toward the little girl and called, "Rocky, it's Mamma!" Rocky lifted her head, but she had heard those words so many times in her dreams that she dismissed it as the howl of the wind. Jamie began to run toward the retreating figures, but just then a patrol car cruised into view on the nearby street. Jamie stopped short and ducked behind a big tree. She heard her heart thumping in her ears as she waited in a haze of indecision. Fifteen minutes passed before she gathered her courage to look around the tree. The street, the cemetery and the parking area were deserted. "Goodbye, Rocky," she whispered.

Chapter 18

Decorating the Tree

Brian dragged the Douglas fir in through the front door, scattering needles on the tile. The children made suggestions and helped to ease the ever-green through the too-narrow door. After a struggle that wore some of the "festive" off of Brian's mood, the tree was stable in its stand. He cut off some of the lower branches and used one of the trimmings to fill an unfortunate gap in the inexpensive tree's symmetry. He screwed it into the trunk and wired it with florist's wire to another branch. "Much better," he congratulated himself.

Lillian hung lights as the children unwrapped the ornaments. Rocky sat on the floor looking at each ornament so familiar to the others. She was fascinated by a set of little porcelain angels. They had golden sashes and elaborate wings. Some held little golden harps, and some had golden halos. Their mouths were all in the shape of an "O". The set also included a bigger, tree-top angel whose costume was more elaborate. Her golden hair hung to her feet, and she had iridescent wings protruding from her shoulders. She held a scroll, and Rocky read "For unto you is born this day," written on it.

"What do you think of them, Rocky? Are they pretty close?" Lillian asked.

"What do you mean?"

"I think you saw angels when you were visited by your grandmother."

Rocky touched the delicate wings and nodded. "But why do they have wings?" she asked.

"To show that they live in heaven. I guess someone once painted angels with wings to show that they live above the Earth like a bird, and the idea caught on. There are places in the scriptures that talk about winged angels and angels flying, so artists give them wings so that we'll know that they are angels."

"I saw the angels more than once," Rocky murmured, but nobody heard.

When the tree was decorated, Josh turned out all other lights in the house except the Christmas tree lights. Lillian lit the special Christmas candles, while Kristen carried a wooden crate with a latching lid into the living room. Katy played "Silent Night" on the piano as Brian sang the words, almost to himself. Rocky crawled to the coffee table like a moth drawn to a light as Lillian opened the wooden crate. She removed the packaging and drew out a tiny wooden stable followed by miniature sheep and cows. Rocky stood by the low table watching as each figure was placed. Gorgeously painted figures were placed beside tiny painted camels at the far edge of the table, as though they were traveling toward the stable. Lillian explained that they did not arrive for some time after the baby was born. When Lillian realized that the story was new to Rocky, she identified shepherds and sheep, Joseph and Mary and a tiny manger. Lillian hung a bright, sparkly star from a lamp that stood near the scene that shone over another angel that held a banner that said "Hosanna" and had a round "O" mouth like the ornaments on the tree. At last Lillian laid the figure of a tiny baby wrapped in bands of cloth, into the cradle of the manger.

Katy began to play again, and this time, everyone but Rocky joined in singing "Silent Night." They knelt in a circle, and Dad said a prayer. He asked Heavenly Father to soften their hearts so that they would always remember

Jesus and to have Him in their countenances. Rocky didn't understand all that was said, but she felt peaceful and reverent and said "amen" with the others at the end of the prayer. Mom served warm cinnamon rolls and cocoa.

When all but Rocky were finished and the mess cleaned up, Brian positioned himself in the big easy-chair facing the tree. Amber climbed into his lap. Rocky still nibbled her cinnamon roll awkwardly as she balanced her cocoa in her other hand.

Brian held out his hand to her, and when she moved closer, he pulled her up opposite Amber, being careful not to make her spill her drink. "What do you think, Rocky? Do you like the Duffin family Christmas tradition?"

Rocky nodded, hardly able to tear her eyes from the angels on the tree. At last, she turned her serious face to Brian and asked, "Why are the angel's mouths shaped like that?"

He looked at the angel on the table and smiled. "They're singing, sweetheart. When Jesus was born on Earth, all the angels in heaven sang for joy." The little girl recognized the name Lillian had given for the One that made the music in the place she had visited.

"Why were they so happy about Jesus being born?"

"They were happy because Jesus is the most important person ever to be born. He is Heavenly Father's real son.

He is the Son of God."

"Why did God's Son get born in a stable? I think he should have been born in the White House or in a Palace."

"Yes, you might think so," he said as he suppressed a smile. "Jesus was born in a stable because God wanted to show all the people of the world that it is good to be humble. Everything in the world is God's, but the things in the world are not what are important. It is the people that are important. God doesn't care if we live in a nice house or a palace or the White House or a little trailer. He only loves and cares about the people inside.

"What did Jesus do when he grew up?" Brian recognized the urgent, hungry undertone in Rocky's voice, and thought for a moment before he answered.

"First, he taught the people how Heavenly Father wanted them to be. He said to love Heavenly Father and to love other people. He told everyone that if they believed in Him and had faith in Him they could live with Him and Heavenly Father forever. He taught us to stop doing bad things and to try every day to be better." Brian paused as he considered the task of condensing the whole of the life of Christ into a simple answer that Rocky could comprehend.

"He also did miracles. When the people were hungry, He fed them. When people were sick, He made them well. When people were diseased, He took away their disease.

He also raised some dead people back to life. He told the people to be kind and humble like little children so that they can go back like little children to their Father in Heaven." He paused again as he saw that Rocky was considering his words and patted her still-rigid back.

"But why was *He* the very *most* important of all?" The rest of the family sat quietly listening to the conversation in the soft glow of the tree.

"Jesus Christ was the most important of all because he had something special to do for all of God's children that we cannot do for ourselves. He was perfect. He never ever did anything wrong. He was always kind, always generous, always doing exactly what God, His Father, wanted Him to do. He was the only perfect person to ever live on the Earth. So He was the only one good enough to do the job that He had to do."

"What was His job?" She whispered the words.

"He died. He suffered pain so terrible that nobody else can even understand. He took the punishment for all the sins and bad things we do and everything that is wrong that anyone ever did or will do. He was perfect, so He had no sins to be punished for, so He took it for all of us. And not only for our sins, He also suffered all of our sadness and grief and loneliness. He suffered for you missing Mom Jamie and your Grandma. He suffered for all our sorrow and everything that makes us sad. He wants everyone to be happy, so we can give our sins and sadness and disappointment to Him, He will take it for us and make us feel better. We just have to ask Heavenly Father to let Jesus take it away from us and follow what he wants us to do, then He will."

"He will take away my sadness about my mom leaving me and never coming back?"

"Yes, Rocky," his voice was tender. "If we ask our kind Father in Heaven to let Jesus take away our sadness, He will."

Rocky sat very still, staring at the little angels. "What happened to Him after that?"

"Then, the people that didn't want others to believe in Him, killed Him." Brian's voice caught in his throat, and he brushed tears off of his cheeks.

"*Why?*" Rocky was incredulous.

They didn't want to lose the things in the world that they loved. They wanted to be rich and important. So they crucified Him by nailing Him to a wooden cross and leaving Him to hang from the nails in His hands and feet until He died. But they didn't know that He needed to die so that He could do the last part of the job He had to do. It was to be resurrected. He came back into his body and now He'll live forever. And because He was resurrected, we also will be resurrected, too!"

"So if I ask Heavenly Father to help me not be sad or mad about my mom anymore, He will?"

"Yes, Rocky"

The little girl rested her head on Brian's chest and sighed. Her eyes were still on the little angels hanging on the Christmas tree. They sat undisturbed for a long time, until the little girl said softly, "*Now I know!*"

Chapter 16

Prayers

Rocky thought about what Brian had said for two days. She wanted to talk to Heavenly Father. She was familiar with family prayers and blessings on the food, and Lillian had taught her to say her prayers. But she said the same words every night. Once, she asked Amber about prayers, and Amber said it was illegal because she wasn't adopted yet. Rocky didn't know if it was all right for her to change her prayer and puzzled on it until at last she asked Lillian.

"Is it illegal for me to talk to Heavenly Father about

Jamie?"

Lillian laughed. "No, No! Of course not! There are rules we have to follow because you're not legally ours yet, but if you want to pray, you sure can. Heavenly Father is just as anxious to hear you as any of His children." Lillian was relieved that the child had finally asked, and she went on to explain, "I like to talk to Heavenly Father alone in my room. I shut the door and kneel down by my bed. Don't you say your prayers every night?"

"I say my prayer, but I want to talk to God."

"'Prayer' is another word for 'talking to God' or 'Heavenly Father.' We call Him by either of those names. Do you need me to help you a little bit?"

Rocky nodded but felt embarrassed as Lillian knelt beside her at her own little bed.

"If you bow your head and close your eyes, it helps you think about who you are talking to. You start by saying 'Heavenly Father'. Then you thank Him for all the good things in your life and for the people you love. Remember, I showed you when you first came to us?"

"Yes, but I always say the prayer you told me that night."

"Oh, I see. Well, you can say whatever you want to say

to Heavenly Father, as long as you are respectful and reverent. I thank Him for giving us Jesus to take away my sins. After you thank Him and ask for forgiveness, tell Him what is bothering you, and ask Him for the things that you need. I ask Him to help others that I care about and to help me to learn to be better. Then, since Jesus is the reason that we can be forgiven, and also the way that our prayers are answered, we say 'I pray in the name of Jesus Christ, Amen.'"

"What does 'Amen' mean?"

"It is a reverent way to finish talking to Heavenly Father."

"Do I have to say it out loud?"

"No, you can say it in your mind, and Heavenly Father can hear you just as well. I usually pray in my mind."

"I want to say it out loud this time so that you can tell me if I do it right. Then I will say it in my mind after that."

"That sounds fine."

Rocky began slowly. "Dear Heavenly Father . . . I am glad I have the Duffins who are nice to me. I am glad I have nice food and a nice house. I like my teacher, Mrs. Trout, and I like my nice clothes and my purse." She paused as though checking a mental list. She continued more seriously, "God? I am feeling a little better about my mother leaving me, but I still cry at night sometimes and when I think of her, I'm really sad. I want to know if my Mom Jamie is okay. So what I am asking you is to help me not be sad anymore. And will you help my Mom Jamie be safe and let me know what," she paused as her voice caught in her throat, "...*happened* to her!" Lillian handed a tissue from the bedside box to the child. "Please let Amber have the pink bike that she wants for Christmas. In the name of Jesus, Amen."

She raised her questioning face to her foster mother. Lillian wiped her eyes quickly and nodded. When she had control of her voice, she said, "That was just fine. That's just the kind of prayer that Heavenly Father pays very careful attention to."

Rocky thought for a moment. "How will He let me know about Mom Jamie being okay?"

"I don't know exactly how He will do it, but He knows the very best way."

Chapter 20

Roxanne Leila Duffin

Rocky took quiet pleasure in the Holiday festivities, but nearly everything was strange and new and nothing compared to the reverence she felt when she thought of the night Brian told her about Jesus. One of the strangest customs, she thought, was that the day before Christmas Eve, the children made tiny houses out of gingerbread and decorated them with all sorts of candy.

Amber asked, “Didn’t you know *anything* about Christmas before you came to us?”

Rocky studied her playmate. "I didn't know *anything* about the real Christmas. I did know about Santa Claus." Her voice took on a note of superiority, "Gingerbread houses don't have anything to do with Christmas *really*."

"They do too!" Amber was defensive. Rocky shook her head, so Amber said, "Mom, *don't* gingerbread houses have to do with Christmas?"

Lillian laughed at the note of triumph in Amber's voice. "No, Amber, actually I have no idea why gingerbread houses and Christmas go together. I think that the idea comes from the story of Hansel and Gretel, and that is certainly *not* a Christmas story." Amber's eyebrows looked like little storm clouds, but she had no other source to appeal to. She didn't comment on Rocky's ignorance after that.

At last it was Christmas Eve and the whole family helped prepare a feast, which they ate in the afternoon. The children wrapped the gifts they had made or bought, that still needed it, in bright paper. When Rocky gave Lillian the gift that she had made for her and Brian, Lillian took it ceremoniously. She read the card aloud, "To Mom Lillian and Dad Brian with *love* from *Roxanne Leila.*"

Lillian noticed with pleasure the changes on the card. "What a pretty name you have! Roxanne Leila suits you well. Thank you for the gift, too; we can hardly wait to open it tomorrow."

Rocky stood very close to Lillian. Her voice quavered as she said, "I want you to call me Roxanne now. I want to *be* Roxanne Leila Duffin." Her eyes were on her feet, but her quick glance was hopeful.

Lillian enfolded the child in her arms and whispered, "Roxanne Leila Duffin sounds wonderful, and Dad and Katy and Kristin and Josh and Amber all think the same."

"Do you think it would hurt Mom Jamie's feelings if she knew?"

"Your mom loved you and took care of you for the first seven years of your life. I think she wanted you to have a new family because she knew she couldn't take good care of you. I think she would be happy that you came to a family who loves you and who you are learning to love." Roxanne nodded with a sigh.

Chapter 21

The Answer

Lillian crossed 'kitchen clean up" off her list when the doorbell rang. Amber screamed, "It's Santa!" as she flung open the door.

Charlene Hollister stood on the doorstep. "Sorry to disappoint you. May I see your Mom or Dad for just a minute?" Roxanne joined Amber in the doorway and Lillian hurried in behind her. "Hello, Rocky. All ready for Christmas?"

"Her name is Roxanne now," Amber informed.

Lillian dried her hands on a dish towel. "There's been a lot going on! Come in out of the cold!"

Charlene stepped in, and Lillian shut the door. "Could I speak with you and Brian privately for just a moment? I know it's Christmas Eve, but I'm going out of town and I think this is important." Roxanne grabbed Lillian's hand and tried to follow her into the living room, but Lillian disengaged her. "Sweety, you and Amber need to finish putting the special dishes away in the hutch. Dad and I need to talk to Miss Charlene."

Brian came downstairs and shook hands with the social worker. "I apologize again for disturbing you on Christmas Eve, but I received a letter at the Department yesterday from Jamie. It was addressed to Rocky, care of the Department of Social Services. I opened it, as the law requires and made a copy for Rocky's file. I think she should have it, but I wanted to let you both decide what was best and when to give it to her." Charlene handed Lillian a sealed envelope addressed to Rocky. "I put it into a fresh envelope and addressed it exactly the way the original was."

Lillian took the letter. "What does it say?"

Well, it's a goodbye letter, and it gives us the legal information we need to finalize your adoption. I really *hate* to read other's mail, so why not just let Rocky share it with you." Lillian nodded, a little embarrassed for asking. Brian looked at the letter over Lillian's shoulder. "Do you think that it would be upsetting to her to get it tonight or would we be better off to wait?"

"Well it does say that Jamie is in jail, and apparently she saw Lillian and Rocky together at the cemetery but was afraid of cops so she hid. But, over all, I think it will help put Rocky's mind at ease. Oh, are you calling her Roxanne now?"

"It was her specific request."

"That is a very good sign. It may symbolize a new start for her."

"Yes, that is exactly what it's about. We understand pretty well what precipitated it, but she is definitely settling in," Brian commented.

The Duffins wished Charlene a merry Christmas and watched her navigate the slippery sidewalk. When she was safely in her car, they shut the door and called Roxanne into the living room. They had to shoo out curious young Duffins, but when they were alone, Lillian invited Roxanne to come and sit on Brian's lap with her. She climbed up opposite her foster-mom. Brian made a comment about two such huge people crushing him to death right before Christmas, and they both laughed.

Then Lillian took Roxanne's hand. "Remember that you prayed that Heavenly Father would let you know that

Jamie was okay? Look what Charlene brought!" She handed the letter to Roxanne's trembling hands. The little girl studied the well-copied address lovingly, and then struggled to open it without damaging the flap of the envelope. She pulled out a sheet of folded notebook paper. She read to herself, mouthing the words.

Dear Rocky,

I am writing to you to say goodby. I am sorry that I left you in the hospital, but I was afrade that they would arrest me for starving you to death. Now I am hoping to get off drugs and booze, but I am doing it the hard way. I am in jail. They arested me for doing drugs and for hurting someone while I was trying to get money for drugs. I know that I am going to prison and I am glad.

I came back to see you when Gramma died. I watched from behind a tree and I could see that you had nice warm clothes and that your hair had grown very long. The lady you were with must be your new mom. I bet she bot you the flours for Gramma's cofin. They were nice.

I wanted you to know that I was okay and that I love you. Never, never, never use drugs or booze. I didn't think they were so bad when I started using when I was 13. I wish I never had them. Don't you ever even try anything like drugs. I lost my little girl because I was too drugged to be a good mom. Don't hate me, but don't forgit me. You are a nice girl. When I get out of prison, I will try to come visit you and I will like to see how you have grown and that you are happy.

Love Jamie

Roxanne stared at the paper for a moment after she read it. She put it to her nose again inhaling the relief it contained in a great sigh. She offered it tentatively to Lillian who held it so they could all see it together. Rocky rested her head on Brian's chest and her tears wet his shirt. He stroked her head as they read the letter.

"It's a very sweet letter, honey. I can tell that she loves you. She just wasn't prepared to be a mom," Brian said.

Roxanne nodded and carefully replaced the letter in the envelope. She slipped off of Brian's lap and laid it under the tree in the area where her gifts were grouped. She smoothed it lovingly and said, "He *did* answer my prayer."

Chapter 22

The Angel's Song

At last the dishes were washed and the kitchen clean. The limp stockings hung from the fireplace mantel, and the tree appeared to be floating on a pond of gifts. Brian gathered the family into the living room as Lillian turned off the lamps and lit the candles around the manger scene. The excited voices subsided into expectant silence.

Brian lifted the heavy Bible from the table behind the little scene and opened it to St. Luke. He looked around at the faces most dear to him gathered in the room, and his eyes rested on Roxanne.

"On this special night, we have our feast to celebrate

all the gifts of the Earth that God has given to us. Then we put our gifts to one another under the tree for tomorrow. Now it is time for us to prepare to give our gifts to the Savior. We start by reading the story of his birth in the Bible." His eyes fell to the page before him and he began to read. "And it came to pass in those days, that there went out a decree from Caesar Augustus, that all the world should be taxed . . ."

Roxanne listened, enthralled by the poetic rhythm of the story and the gentle cadence of his voice. Fresh questions rose in her mind, but she did not want to break the magic of the peace that filled her. She imagined the fearful shepherds and the rejoicing angels. She wondered if the star that shone was a star that had stayed in the sky or if it disappeared later on. She thought of Mary cradling her baby in her arms and then laying him in the little manger. She knew that the manger must have been pillowed with soft straw and probably had a little blanket over it so that it wouldn't scratch. She imagined herself kneeling beside the manger, touching the baby's face. She sighed when the reading was over and Brian closed the Bible.

He said, "Now each of us will take a turn in thanking Jesus for what he did for us. Roxanne, it can be any way you want, even silently in your mind. We go from oldest to youngest, and I'll start, then Mom, then Kristen, Katy and Josh. Then we'll let Amber go and Roxanne last because she was last to join our family.

I will thank Jesus by not getting mad when I'm driving anymore. I will not call people knuckle-heads, idiots, or fools even if they do cut me off or tailgate. I will control my temper and ignore all offences that I can safely ignore." The little smile on his face belied his serious tone.

"Yay!" Lillian laughed. "I never thought you would give up on the knuckleheads, idiots and fools!"

"Well, it's your turn, darling. What have you got in mind for *yourself*?"

Lillian became serious and finally said she would remember to say her prayers every morning and be more patient with the children.

Kristen wanted to include more unpopular kids in her circle of friends. Katy played a beautiful Christmas song on the piano and explained that her gift was to bring more beautiful music into the world. Josh wanted to be a better student, and not make Mom nag him. When Amber had finished singing "Silent Night" without missing a single word, Brian turned to Roxanne. "If you just want to think it in your mind, that's okay."

Roxanne took a deep breath and shook her head. "I want to do something."

"Great! Do you want some help?"

Roxanne shook her head again. She went to the Christmas tree and touched a little "singing" angel thoughtfully. "I know the Angel's Song." She spoke simply without shyness. "And I want to sing it for you."

She closed her eyes and began the song. At first it was soft and almost tuneless, but soon the sweet voice swelled, and she began putting words to it. "I sing about Jesus because he took away my sadness. Jesus! Jesus! He hung on the cross so that I would not be sad anymore. Everyone will live forever because He died for us!

Her song floated and swelled, following an unexpected, yet beautiful tune. "I love Him! He let me hear the Angels singing. He gave me my new Mom and Dad and Katy and Kristen and Josh and Amber. He answered my prayer that Jamie was okay, and He told her to write me a new letter. Someday I will see Jamie and tell her that Jesus took away my sadness. I love you, Jesus! Someday I will go back to Heaven and kiss your hands and feet where the nails went in. I will say, 'Thank you! Thank you!' I want you to hug me and say, 'You are my little girl.' Jesus, Jesus! I love you, I love you!"

The child let the last note fade into silence, but even then it seemed to float in the air. When she opened her eyes, she realized that they were all looking at her and shyness returned like a cloak. She said very softly, "That is like the angels' song."

At once the family folded her in an embrace that melted away the last of the walls that had separated them.

ക ക ക

Though famous artists have bowed to thunderous applause in opera houses, though orchestras have thrilled audiences with the beauty of their music, and though many train and practice until they achieve technical perfection, they are yet lacking. For never has there been a song more divine than was heard in that small parlor on Christmas Eve.

For she sang of Him – He, who created the Earth and the star that brightened the sky at His birth. He made the fish that He ate and the water He walked upon. He made the tree that was fashioned into a cross and the stone that became His tomb. He fashioned the sheep and the shepherds. All these things, we see and love and remember. But only those who have tasted a bit of the bitterness He knew and have given it back to Him to keep, know the song. Rarely, since that night over two thousand years ago, has the veil been lifted just enough for those on Earth to hear the Angels' Song.

The End

Made in the USA
Charleston, SC
21 November 2009